LINGUA FRANCA

Miles Platting is pulled from the ruins of a shipwreck into a world where no one will speak to him. The founder of *Lingua Franca* — a naming rights agency committed to rechristening every UK town after a corporate sponsor — Miles recounts the story of his quest for linguistic supremacy to anyone who'll listen. Confined to a hospital bed in a deathly quiet ward, he wants to find his colleagues and be reunited with his true love. But in doing so, he must confront his most deeply held convictions, in a world where the spoken word has been replaced with silence.

WILLIAM THACKER

LINGUA FRANCA

Complete and Unabridged

ULVERSCROFT
Leicester

First published in Great Britain in 2016 by
Legend Press Ltd
London

First Large Print Edition
published 2017
by arrangement with
Legend Press Ltd
London

A catalogue record for this book is available
from the British Library.

ISBN 978-1-4448-3122-1

Published by
F. A. Thorpe (Publishing)
Anstey, Leicestershire

Set by Words & Graphics Ltd.
Anstey, Leicestershire
Printed and bound in Great Britain by
T. J. International Ltd., Padstow, Cornwall

This book is printed on acid-free paper

1

BLUE SKY THINKING

Shortly is an excellent word. It can mean whatever you want it to mean. *A member of our team will get back to you shortly.* When exactly? Shortly. *Imminent* is too much. An imminent announcement. Imminent death. Maybe if your death were due *shortly*, you wouldn't mind so much. I like *shortly*. There are three words that should never have made it into English. The first is *moist*. It sounds bad in any context. The second is *phlegm*. Just because. And third, worst of all, is *flaccid*. Flaccid should go. Flaccid should do one.

'Can anyone hear me? Hello?'

At the same time, there are words which ought to be used more. Like *ought*. *Flummox* is cool. *Hubbub* is great. *Genteel. Marigold. Curmudgeon. Lackadaisical?* Too much. *Rigmarole* is a weird one. Have I been put through a rigmarole? I think I have.

'Hello? It's Miles Platting! Anyone there?'

I can still remember the important things. I know I made a point of waving my arms

— an SOS signal — long in advance of getting hit. I was standing there, a lone man on an island, under a deluge. It seemed to happen in an instant; I opened my eyes and couldn't tell what was water and what was blood. We had a fortress, a town-within-a-town, and then it happened. The sea punished us for having built with cheap plywood. All around me there's junk from the unit base: broken teapots and furniture legs, corrugated iron and splintered wood. I'm surrounded by objects that have no place underground: a garden gnome, porcelain rabbits. There's a kettle with its spout missing, a car boot sale gone wrong. Words come into my head for no reason, words like *rigmarole*. Most of the time, I don't really think of anything. I think of Kendal, and then I have to think of something else.

The escape plan is weather-dependent. If the rain loosens up the rocks, I'll reach up and climb my way out. The extent of my movement is limited to looking left or right. I'm on a live TV pause. To keep myself entertained I've taken to counting woodlice. One woodlouse . . . two woodlice . . . I should think of a name for the slug crawling next to my shoulder. Bertie, perhaps. Bertie the slug. A *slug* isn't a great name for a living creature. It should be something more

2

onomatopoeic: a *slimer*.

I get a sense that someone's a few feet above my head, picking their way through the rocks. All I can rely on is the searchlight, which does its best to shine upon tin cans and clothes pegs. Every object except me. I can see its movement on the rocks — it snakes in and out of each gap except the one in which I'm stuck. I find myself cursing whoever's in charge of the light, and wishing they would give it to someone else.

'I'm down here! Miles Platting!'

The light no longer shines. I can just about manage a bad-tempered wheeze, the slow pull of an accordion that stretches all my limbs. It adjusts my body so that I'm now facing the slime of a rock, something I'd spent hours getting away from. Above ground, they'll reconvene at what remains of the unit base. If Nigel's around, he'll reproach them for not having better planning procedures. They'll talk about the logistical difficulties in moving all the rubble. They'll analyse historical case studies that suggest I'm already dead. They might even place a stone on top of me. They ought to keep searching until I've run out of air bubbles, or my stomach's finished eating itself. I might have become a sensation, a running media story with everyone asking where I've gone and whether I'll be found. I'll be a hero on the basis of my existence. Or maybe no one will care. What if no one cares? What if there aren't any cameras? It would be a shame if no one organised a night-time vigil or a 'pray for Miles' campaign. There is a process in the event of my death. There is a prepared statement, which expresses shock at the sudden manner of my passing. It urges caution, since the police need time to conduct an investigation. There will be a media strategy designed to maximise the goodwill of the nation. Lingua Franca will be closed the next day; a minute's silence will be staged. The statement will conclude that murder has no place in a modern society, or indeed an ancient one. Nothing will stop Lingua Franca from exacting its duties. Our determination to carry on is unshakeable. A decision about Miles Platting's successor will be made in due course.

Something drops in a heap: a coil of rope. The sound of a drill comes next. From my angle, which amounts to a gap in the ceiling, I can see a couple of men in fluorescent jackets with torches on their heads.

'Hello! I'm down here! I'm Miles Platting!'

I can see one of them put a finger to their lips like I'm going to cause an avalanche. Their method is to remove one rock at a time. One of them snips the tangled metal with a pair of cutters. The other is attached to a bungee harness; he descends until I can almost touch him. I lift my arms like a baby in a high chair, waiting for him to carry me free. 'Thank you!'

He looks at me and says nothing. What a pro! I cling to him. I say what a nightmare it's been, how I've been stuck here for god-knows-how-long with nothing to do but lick the rainwater and talk to slugs. I cut up my leg and I probably have blood running down my shin. Nothing's broken, I think. I fell from the front of the boat and I must have landed before everything came down on me; I feel entombed, almost. Apart from that, I'd like to know if the Israeli-Palestinian conflict has been resolved, and who won the Ryder Cup. He smiles at my questions but gives no answer. He yanks on his rope and we rise together. I'm leaving behind the underworld. So long, twisted metal. *Arrividerci*, jagged rocks. I'll miss you, Bertie. Above me, I can see rescue helmets and thick, grey cloud. Then suddenly I'm out into the half-light. I blink and splutter like someone's turned on a light and woken me up. I wince, which is the most comfortable thing to do. There are ambulance staff and a crowd of people I've never seen — they see that I'm standing upright and they clap their hands. I'm released from the belt and held in place. I don't have much strength in my legs — the baby is learning to walk. I'm guided down the pebble verge. Someone puts a towel over my shoulders. All around me there's strewn clothes and litter. I can see broken porcelain which probably comes from our kitchen sink. I recognise the portable toilet in its new context: floating in the sea. Dotted along the shoreline I can see red and yellow metal sheets — the fragments of each shipping container. The table tennis table is broken. Most of the sleeping pods have been wrecked completely. A mess is what it is.

'Where is everyone? Are they alright?'

No one seems to know. Or no one's going to tell me anything. They take me along the shoreline; they accompany me on my limp. I notice the remains of our kitchen: the fridge and the cooker are gathered in a heap. The sea remains calm. It doesn't hold itself responsible. On the wooden dock, someone's put a line of shoes. I can see a red Adidas trainer belonging to Darren, and Nigel's leather Oxfords. I can't see anything of Kendal's. I suppose that's a good thing.

I catch sight of myself in the ambulance wing mirror. My hair is beyond the out-of-bed look, beyond ironic. My normal instinct would be to shield my face from any cameras. We're supposed to be indestructible. We're Lingua Franca. Look on our works, ye Mighty, and despair! I'm not sure that really matters anymore. I'm not sure we even exist.

'Can someone tell me where everyone is?'

They open the ambulance doors and help me clamber inside. I'm lifted onto the thin, hard mattress, which reminds me of being in a school medical room. I'm glad to hear the ignition.

⋆ ⋆ ⋆

I'm taken somewhere, but I don't feel conscious enough to know what's going on. I'm unloaded onto a trolley and suddenly we're moving at speed. In a small medical room they inspect me, feed me and dress me in a blue patient gown. I can tell by their smiles that I'm welcome, but no one says anything. It's like I'm a murderer who's been caught. It seems I'm entitled to free medical care but the silent treatment too.

The doctor has shoulder-length grey hair and reminds me of a grey squirrel. It's a large permed hair-do, and I wonder for a moment whether concussion can transport you to the 1980s. She retrieves a sheet from the holder on the wall and lays it fresh on the table. She finds a pen and concentrates on her

7

handwriting, as if good handwriting were the most important thing in the world. She lifts the sheet so I can look at the words.

Miles, welcome to Furness General Hospital. We're going to help you get better.

She puts a dot where she wants a reply. She gestures for me to write what I'm thinking. There's enough white space to accommodate a full exchange.

'Where's Kendal?'

She looks at me like I've caused offence; I've entered a sacred building and said the worst thing possible (which happens to be anything in the English language). She turns around and starts tending to another patient, who looks determined to sleep, but unable to. I can feel myself frowning as I write on the page.

Where's Kendal?

The doctor smiles over-animatedly. She seems glad about my participation. She takes back the sheet.

You can see Kendal when you're better.

She looks at me and expects me to write

something. She wants me to play the game. I lean as far as my ache will allow. I draw something.

>:-(

I don't relinquish the pen. I write in big letters.

Do you know where she is?

The doctor confers with a nurse; I notice the movement of their hands. They seem to rely upon hand gestures and body language. The doctor employs some sort of finger spelling. The nurse nods.

I lean up in bed. 'Hello?'

Each of them make a shushing sound. They pull the curtain to conceal me from the ward. I'm enclosed. Trapped again. I feel like I want to get up and run. I look at the monitor which displays my heart rate bleeping faster. The doctor slips through the curtain and puts a hand to my forehead. She unscrews a lid and empties some pills into a glass of water. The doctor writes what appears to be a longer sentence or two.

Kendal's fine. But you're not allowed any visitors until you're better.

I'm fine.

You're ill, Miles.

This time I say it. 'I'm fine.'
   She shakes her head. I'm a bad patient.
   'What is this place? Where is everyone?'
   She tells me again — in writing — that I'm ill. She tells me that my memory's bad and I should write down everything I can remember.

As soon as you're better, we can help you find Kendal.

She offers me the pen. She looks at me, waiting for something. I have the pen, and apparently that's all I need. I might as well start from the beginning.

2

THE CAT THING

I first conceived of Lingua Franca at a post-colonialism lecture in Wonga, the county town of Worcestershire. The guest speaker, Kendal, gave a presentation titled 'Geographical Renaming from Abyssinia to Zaire'. She listed historical examples of renamed settlements, de-Stalinised towns, and asked whether St Petersburg by any other name would smell as sweet. Stalingrad, Stalinabad, Stalinstadt, Stalinogorsk. Peking, Constantinople, Danzig. I listened to everything Kendal said, and I decided that the Czech Republic would be infinitely cooler if it was still called Bohemia. Out of this came Lingua Franca.

'Good afternoon, sir. My name is Eden and I'm calling from Lingua Franca. Is the person in charge of the council available? Oh, it's just about naming rights for the town. You see, here at Lingua Franca we specialise in increasing the revenue of town councils by . . . okay, not to worry, sir.'

I listen for anything which deviates from

the script — we're Lingua Franca, naming rights specialists, and we're here to partner with your town and reduce your debt burden. Does that sound like something you might be interested in, sir? The lads — and they're all lads — must always follow the script. To some extent they can develop their own style. Some of them wear headsets, which allows them to use both hands on the keyboard. The majority like to stand when the call is happening. They know when I'm listening; the tone of their voice hardens. They're not going to let me down.

The emergency alarm takes the form of an intermittent beep. It stops the whole office from performing their duties — you can't make a sales call when there's a loud beeping noise all around you. When it sounds, most of the guys look up from their small, note-ridden desks as if to say *What do we do? Is this a reprieve? Do we get to smoke and pretend we do something else for a living?* They look at me, and they look at Nigel; after all, we founded this company, and we tell them what to do. Nigel claps his hands and tells them to evacuate via the stairs.

What impresses me about Nigel is how calmly he locks the panic room. We sometimes share it with a finance company, but only if they get here fast. Otherwise we shut the door. We like to entomb ourselves. There is a small window, which gives the faint impression of freedom. The glass is strong enough to withstand a hail of rocks. In fairness, it can only be breached if someone is determined to kill you. They'd have to fly a remote-controlled helicopter and somehow shoot bullets from its undercarriage.

Nigel talks on the phone to security; he nods, which means something's happening. He puts down the receiver. 'Guy with a knife.'

The routine is so familiar that it no longer makes me nervous. It's boring, more than anything. The lads are standing in the car park. They like alarm drills because it gives them a chance to smoke. They don't realise that I'm watching them — they push each other around and wrestle. It makes me worry that they behave in such a toe-the-line way when they know I'm watching, but like animals when they think I'm not. I serve a function in their lives: I authorise their pay cheques, write their references and manage their self-esteem. My power is conditional. From the window you can see how the modern part of Stella Artois has been planned. The roads form a rectangular grid — a Belgian waffle in town form. There is something calculated about it. There is a section of raised motorway and a polluted canal. If your eye is drawn to anything, the shopping centre is the obvious thing. The roads seem to converge towards the shopping centre, making it the cathedral. It has grown ugly, the town. On the horizon is a small neighbourhood called Stella Artois Old Town. Here, the street pattern is less sensible. There is a hint of picture book England: a church, some timbered pubs and a bowling green. The residents have a fondness for conservationist groups, duck ponds and anti-miscegenation laws. I dislike Stella Artois Old Town.

Everyone begins to regenerate, slowly coming back into the world as the person they once were. I only have to look at Nigel for something to happen — he's my yo-yo, and I unfurl him when I want. He does the clapping. He shouts, 'Gather round, guys.' Everyone in the company assembles in a circle. We begin the *expression session*. Nigel points to the head of operations. 'Ops! How's your week going?'

She says 'Good, thank you,' with no added joke or banter, no tacit acknowledgement that in our preferred world none of us would be standing here talking about the daily processes of a naming rights agency. 'We had constructive dialogue with Carlisle, who want to rename one of their car parks. We've got a couple of automotive brands interested in that one.'

'Tell them we'll get back to them *shortly*.'

Everyone nods. No one wants to look uninterested. 'And our highlight for the week was the Friday night social, which was super-fun.'

Nigel smiles and thanks the operations manager. Then he turns to the head of sales. 'Sales — what are we forecasting for November?' Nigel has his pen primed, ready to make a note.

'We estimate thirteen.'

'Including Stevenage?'

'Including Stevenage.'

'What happened to Motherwell?'

'Motherwell's gone cold.'

'Pity, because Mothercare would have been a good match.'

'It would have made sense.'

'Thank you, sales. Who am I missing? Localisation.'

The head of localisation talks about the rebranding of Skegness, which was six months ago. It's now called Vue, after the cinema company. 'We're in the process of renaming Skegness Pier, which is going to be called Vue Pier, but possibly with Vue spelt *view*, subject to focus group polling.'

Around the circle there's a positive

murmur. 'I think it sounds classy,' someone says.

'Thank you, localisation.' Nigel points at the tech team, and we listen to nothing anyone understands. We go round the circle, which includes the accounts department, publicity and general admin. When it gets to my turn, my only contribution is to remind everyone to empty the fridge so it doesn't start to smell. Everyone seems to find this funny. I'm the warm, fuzzy segment at the end of the six o'clock news.

'Thank you, Miles. That's a wrap, folks!'

It starts again, the noise: the sound of telesales men getting impatient, the photocopier scanning something, the huge server trying to out-hum the air conditioner, the absence of music, the measured tone in everyone's voice. The lads get back on it, reconfiguring their work face and lifting the receiver. They all know the rules — they're hungry salesmen and they need to eat. I often forget their names.

* * *

'I don't hate you, Miles. You're just in charge of the most appalling cultural phenomenon in decades. You've made it your personal duty to kill the English language and replace it with

16

corporate fluff. You've taken something beautiful and made it ugly.'

'Do you still want to have lunch?'

'Only if you're going to apologise.'

'For what?'

'Ruining the world.'

Kendal has been holding a pen while making the point. I thought the pen was going to snap. She doesn't understand what it takes to maintain the competitiveness of a multimillion pound business. She doesn't care about these things, and wouldn't care even if I gave her a ten-hour lecture on its importance. We both like to argue for the necessity of our existence while being secretly jealous of the other. 'Woe, destruction, ruin and decay,' she says. 'The worst is death, and death will have his day.'

'I'm not listening.'

'Are you ready to die?' Kendal says, but not like a murderer might say it. She enters the kitchen and lights a cigarette on the hob. She peers through the bulletproof kitchen window and says, 'I don't want you getting killed. As much as you fucked up our lives, I do care about you . . . a bit.'

'I'll be fine.'

'Jesus, you can't even open a fucking window in this place.'

'Pull it towards you.'

She gets it open. She leans her head and blows out smoke. She looks at the courtyard, no doubt reflecting on her hatred of the compound. It's the most expensive development in Stella Artois, and certainly the most security conscious. The apartments have perimeter walls with sharp, metal spikes. The courtyard gravel amplifies the sound of footsteps. Hidden in the lamp posts are surveillance cameras. A nightwatchman sits watching snooker in a security box. The concessions to beauty come in pastiche-form: wisteria on the walls, spurious Latin inscriptions. The development wants to belong to every period of history except this one. 'For in that sleep of death what dreams may come,' Kendal says.

Ptolemy follows me into the kitchen. Ptolemy has thick grey fur. You can run your hands through it. I wouldn't do well with a short-haired cat. I wouldn't like to feel its spine. Ptolemy looks at me and I can sense what she's thinking. You bastard. She hasn't been fed all day. 'No one fed you, did they?' I find myself saying. I scrape jellied meat into the bowl. She sniffs at the food. If she were a human she'd be a demanding child, unaware of her privilege and suspicious of giving anything a try. 'Come on, baby.' She licks the food and all is forgiven. 'Good girl.'

Kendal stubs her cigarette on the window ledge. 'Is this part of your decline? The cat thing.'

'I've been doing this for years. You just weren't paying attention.'

'It's part of your decline.'

The noise of the boiling kettle scares Ptolemy and she dashes to the living room. Kendal begins to moan about teaching and the educational standards in Stella Artois. She's tired of explaining the difference between *you're* and *your*. Over the years, Kendal has undergone various incarnations: the student idealist, the almost-mum to our almost-children, and finally, the deflated mid-life Kendal — the one who teaches English. We used to joke about how Kendal filled our moral hardship quota, which gave me license to do evil. She took one for the team. I don't have any backup now. No one's doing good on my behalf. I'm evil-plus.

'Do you think we should move in together?' she says.

'No.'

'It can be completely soulless, Miles. I can just live off your money and we can have sex with whoever we want.'

'I think that's what happened the first time.'

It ended like most of these things do. It got to the point where neither of us wanted the same things. I didn't want to have children; Kendal didn't want to support a naming rights consultant responsible for the death of the English language. In her heart, Kendal doesn't want to come home. The pragmatic mind, which weighs the importance of mortgage repayments, might decide I'm worth a second chance. The heart says no.

On the table is the Lingua Franca brand catalogue, the 48-page booklet that details our creative vision. The first page says: *In the beginning there was the word.* Kendal smiles as she turns the pages. She shakes her head at the image of a waterfall juxtaposed with the word. MoneySuperMarket. 'Miles, Miles, Miles. You were beautiful once.' She feels my old tweed jacket wrapped around the chair. She looks at the bookshelf for evidence of my decline. 'Oh dear.' She picks up a copy of *Naked Lunch* and shakes her head. 'This isn't you. You're not a Burroughs fan.'

'You don't know what I read.'

'You're a slow reader, that's what you are. Where are all the marketing books about ripping people off?'

'With the books about bitter ex-wives.'

'*Current* wives.' She fondles the key in the bureau lock. 'Unless you've got some divorce papers in here.' She spots something else. 'Oh, what?'

'Stop looking at my books!'

'When was the last time you read Audre Lorde?'

'There's no time.'

'I know you, Miles Platting. You're not a feminist. Are you trying to impress a lady?' I feel naked. 'You shouldn't be allowed to own that book. You can't do all the shit you do, then try and *own* Audre Lorde. Sure, you can put Lorde on your bookshelf but that doesn't mean you own it. Miles Platting, destroyer of worlds. Likes Audre Lorde.'

'Why don't you take some books home? I know you're hard-up at the moment. Put it in a doggy bag.'

She sticks up a middle finger. In these encounters, we like to road-test our best material. She doesn't mind talking about her poverty, but not to be reminded of it. She puts Audre Lorde back, a different spot to where she found it. She knows that she's ruined my alphabet. 'Oh, Miles, Miles, Miles.'

'Kendal, Kendal.'

'I'd better go.'

She looks in the mirror and pretends to be uninterested in her reflection. She used to have long hair but now she has a short pixie cut where most of the effort goes into coiffuring the front. It's a haircut that says *fuck you, Miles*. The act of leaving requires my assistance. The access code is 1985. It was originally 1984, but Kendal advised that 1984 is the first code that burglars try, so long as they're literate. She looks at me. The only word I can think of is pity.

'Don't get killed.'

'I won't.'

Ptolemy watches from the piano. She likes to watch people from a great height.

'My class has exams tomorrow. I think they might fail on purpose.'

'It'll be fine.'

'Wish me luck.'

'You wish me luck as well.'

'For what?'

'Staying alive.'

'It's not a contest.'

It goes on like this, and it turns out that neither of us wishes good luck upon the other.

'I don't want to say goodbye like this.'

'How should we say it?'

'Say something nice.'

I explain that if I could do anything, I'd buy Paris and change its name to Kendal. She allows herself to blush.

3

THE ENGLISH CHICAGO

It begins with a sweeping shot of the ocean. On the horizon are the rusting cranes of Barrow-in-Furness. Everything looks cold. It's hard to decide whether the sea looks green or grey. The clouds have no problem with raining on the town. There's not much in the way of action, besides a slow-motion ship coming into the slipway. The next thing in sight is a fishing boat, from which it's possible to make out the town as a silhouette. All you're meant to know is that Barrow is a place, and it's distant — unattached. None of us need to worry. This is as close as any of us will get.

'This is Barrow,' the narrator says. 'It used to be one of the proudest towns in Britain.' We accelerate, moving into the town. We reach land, and the rows of houses become dense and repetitive. We can see the town for what it is — a grid of terraced houses and a church in the middle. 'Life in Barrow isn't what it used to be,' the narrator says. We see a checkout girl in a supermarket; she's scanning items and shaking her head. It's not the Barrow she once knew. An elderly man is waiting to cross the road but none of the cars are willing to stop. What will bring Barrow back to life? If the video is to be believed, what's missing is the magic. Not money, of course. It's just the magic that's missing. The images come faster now. A recycling skip is piled with wet cardboard. The playground is empty — a swing rocks back and forth. Next is a young boy. He's bouncing a bright orange ball in slow motion. This is the only way any of us will get to experience Barrow. We're watching from afar. We might be able to visit when the magic happens, and people start smiling, but not until then. 'Barrow deserves better,' the narrator says. 'Barrow deserves Birdseye.' Suddenly there is colour. The seagulls are racing home. A little boy is walking hand-in-hand with his sister. It's a montage of images in which women laugh, children run around and nothing bad appears to have ever happened. A crumbling school building is being painted white. The checkout girl is smiling. The town seems content with itself. What was ugly can become beautiful in an instant. Peace is all around us. The slogan says:

Birdseye-in-Furness: The Promise of a Brighter Barrow.

There's a problem with Barrow, but it can be fixed. You just need to change the name to Birdseye. Everyone applauds once the credits roll. The reaction is the same as ever — the same as Skegness, Skelmersdale, and all the others that came before. Just like Runcorn and just like Redcar — everyone applauds, as if the video can hear us. I make eye contact with the front row — the town council representatives of Barrow-in-Furness. What stops them from smiling is their basic instinct, which tells them that Barrow-in-Furness should always be called Barrow-in-Furness. It shouldn't be known by any other name.

'As you can see, we've matched Barrow with a brand that recognises its maritime history. The naming rights will cover all maps, road signs, transport timetables, public buildings, digital media and more. Members of the media will be duty bound to substitute the name Barrow-in-Furness for its replacement, Birdseye-in-Furness. Yes, there will be a certain amount of residual anger. The typical cooling off period for the public is six to eight weeks. A critical mass should begin referring to the new town by its brand name after about three years. A unanimous transferral of loyalty from one name to another can take generations. With the right brand, though, it can happen a lot sooner. And we believe we've selected the right brand at the right time.'

In my attempts to describe what we've just watched, I sound almost professional — a scholar. They must imagine that I'm qualified in something other than talking-a-good-game, or selling town names for a competitive rate. I'm not a linguistics professor, sadly. I have no grounding in the study of language other than my ability to sell it. I'm not a professor of anything. I'm a man with an idea. I got some money from an angel investor. Nigel liked the concept and took a nominal salary. We got a sales team of cheap school-leavers and outsourced technical work to a company in Bangalore. Our first clients came along — bankrupt town councils like Congleton and Kettering. Then came Didcot and Dudley, Barnstable and Penrith. All of them wanted to make a statement that change is coming and renewal is on the way. You just have to change your name to Birdseye. 'It's not just the town name that can be sold. We offer a premium package for the right to sponsor street names, public squares and neighbourhoods. Here at Lingua Franca, our service is tailored to the exact needs of every client.' I've been practising this for months. Sometimes I spend twenty minutes in front of the mirror, talking aloud about the benefits of naming rights. It's easy to make the argument at this point; the town officials start to think about their property values, and how they might retire in peace and comfort. Lingua Franca will make your town rich. Businesses will invest, wages will rise. The town will feature in property supplements. No one could possibly conclude that selling Barrow's naming rights won't result in prosperity for all. They're getting it now. They're beginning to see what Lingua Franca can do. They weren't fully sold at first — more like half-in, half-out — but now they're getting it. We can all get paid. We can exchange the habits of a lifetime for something more tangible — money. Barrow-in-Furness whisper among themselves, conferring like game show contestants. Without Lingua Franca, they wouldn't know how to promote Barrow, and how to position themselves in the marketing world. They probably don't understand what's going on.

'Thank you very much,' the councillor says. 'I think we're ready to proceed.'

Change is coming. By the morning, we'll have another red pin on our British Isles map.

The next stage is to take them into the office, a process designed to convince them we know what we're doing — which, in fairness, we do. They're welcome to step into the office and review the procedure by which their town will be branded and sold to the world. The office itself has been designed with the intention of relaxing everyone. There is a floor-to-ceiling image of a woodland path. It gives the impression — completely contrary to our business activities — that we have anything to do with planet earth. You can hear everyone typing when it's quiet like this. Normally, the office has a natural rhythm, which doesn't allow for silence. There is a massive clock on the wall, which everyone pretends not to notice. I permit the town officials to walk around the office, doing as they please, which involves looking at the sales team and waiting for some kind of clue, some kind of guilt. The clients don't actually pay for this service — I've checked the terms of usage — but it makes sense to allow the illusion.

'Barrow will be at the vanguard of modern town branding,' I say aloud. 'Look what we did for Watford.'

It's only when I raise my voice, and reaffirm the premise of Lingua Franca, that our friends from Barrow begin to animate. 'Is there a security risk?'

'Not in the slightest.'

The councillor doesn't really know what

he's looking for. He walks around, peering under the tables. He probably thinks he's going to find something suspicious. The councillor's distinguishing feature is his creased forehead, which overhangs — *protrudes* is better — so that his nose and lips seem squashed-in. You get the sense he might ram you with his forehead before he shakes your hand.

'Looks good, that,' the councillor says, pointing at the screen. From his accent you can tell the man is from somewhere in the north. Somewhere rich, though. The incongruous north. We stand around a computer, looking at an image of Barrow-in-Furness. The designer has done an excellent job. It looks nothing like Barrow-in-Furness.

Nigel emerges to say, 'It has an alpine quality — a kind of Sydney Harbour, but with an alpine quality.' Nigel explains the next stage of the process, which is the launch. We'll arrive in Barrow, christen it Birdseye, and keep a safe distance from the town. There will be a naming ceremony with dignitaries in attendance. It's a circus, yes, but a highly profitable one. The circus needs a ringleader, and our duty will be to stand in front of a crowd and herald the Birdseye revolution as the best thing ever to happen to Barrow.

I introduce the officials to the project

delivery team, whose emphasis is on design, content and PR. These people are graduates, desperate for work and always keen to show me what a good job they're doing. There's an intern, who is keen to smile at every opportunity. It's not that she's friendly; she just knows who I am. This is disconcerting. It makes me think she would do anything for money. The geeks and creatives work in tandem to create slogans and pictures. The purpose of their labour is to convince the world that Birdseye is worth visiting and worth our attention. It's not Barrow, for one thing. All of them are plugged into our mindset — that town sponsorship means money, and money means happiness.

The councillor continues to twirl the key fob chain. It's a temporary pass, and he shouldn't be twirling it. He looks at the bank of telesales staff like it's something he's never seen before. 'Ah, the engine room,' he says. The sales team want to be left alone. No one wants to engage in faux-banter when you've got calls to make. They degrade themselves in exchange for money. They deserve the decency of being left alone. Suddenly, everyone's selling at the same time. It's hard to decipher the words. It's reminiscent of commentators getting excited as the horses reach the final furlong.

'Good afternoon, you're speaking to Eden at Lingua Franca. We are the UK's number one naming rights agency. Who can I speak to about naming rights for the town?' Eden has the ability to bullshit on demand. He's a seasoned performer when it comes to bullshit. The tone is sharp — it's the sound of someone who's spent ages perfecting his voice. It's a kind of professional register that doesn't exist in normal life — no one would speak like this unless instructed to do so. 'Here at Lingua Franca we provide hassle-free naming rights solutions. What we offer is a comprehensive end-to-end solution — we will partner with your town and give it the exposure it deserves.' I find myself nodding, without realising, until it becomes apparent that Nigel is looking at me. 'Would it be a good idea if I popped you some details in an email, sir? I can promise you — it's a real thriller.' Eden can do a good job of sounding enthusiastic. The thing about Eden is that you never quite know if he's going to have a breakdown. He doesn't live for the simple pleasure of getting a pay slip, which guarantees drinking money. He wants to exist and engage outside of these walls. It's a credit to Eden that he ever turns up at all. If you look closer, his left eye is beginning to flicker. He doesn't appear to have been sleeping much. Eden has weathered the worst of the Lingua Franca experience. His relationship with civilisation is to tolerate things that do him harm. He will only surrender when he can't get up anymore. For now, he's still standing.

'It's a well-oiled machine,' the councillor says, doing his best to get Eden's attention, which must be irritating for Eden. It's hard enough for Eden to concentrate on his lines without having some ignorant fool leaning over. Eden is able to look up and half smile while remaining focused on the call. It's quite a feat to be able to manage both things at once. He manages to put the same effort into pleasantries as he does the phone calls. He once told me that it's a relief to come here. At home, all he does is argue. 'He's good,' the councillor says, which Eden would have heard. By the time Eden has finished with the call, and risen from his seat, it seems that half the room is watching him.

'Who was that, Eden?'

'Basingstoke.'

'What are they saying?'

'They want to change their name to something vibrant. An energy drink, or something.' The sales board features a grid of names and roman numerals. Eden rubs the ink with a sponge. He writes another digit in his column, another stay of execution.

'Have you got the direct debit?'

'It's done.'

There is a holler. Some of the lads congratulate Eden; some of them ignore everything. Nigel offers a hand. Everyone takes it in turns. Here we are — a functioning business. The councillor doesn't offer a hand but he smiles from a distance. It will make the councillor feel less vulnerable to know that some other town is joining the party. It's happening. Eden is unmoved by it all. He's reluctant to accept the handshakes. He doesn't seem to care, aside from the simple numbing pleasure in making a sale. It's a balm. He has the ability to live for another month. Eden picks up the phone and dials another number. The sales team is required to stay until six o'clock, which is later than everyone else — except the cleaners, who are just getting started. Then it all subsides and everyone returns to their desk and realigns their work-face.

Someone calls Grimsby to find out whether it wants to change its name to Qatar Airways.

* * *

The after hours involve strategic planning, which essentially means listening to Nigel talk about how things ought to be different. This is the time of day when ideas emerge. It's clear-the-air time, when the day's successes and failures can be viewed for what they are. It's also when we gossip in the only way certain types of men can do: we discuss who's fat and who ought to throw themselves off the roof. Through the glass we can see Eden sitting at his desk, a Gormley statue. He likes to stay behind afterwards. It's the only time of day that he's able to check his emails. Eden invites suspicion by his own intelligence. Something must have gone wrong.

'I think he's been drinking,' Nigel says.

'How do you know?'

'I could smell it on his breath. He's probably drunk right now.'

Within these walls, no one can hear us. I've tested it from the other side. This is our glass incubator. Eden looks at us and raises a hand to say goodbye. He does everything in a swift, uncomplicated manner. The way in which he grabs his coat from the rail is for the purpose of getting out fast. I tell Nigel that I'm going for a walk. It's satisfying to be able to step into the office and observe a quiet room, absent of telephone chatter. The entire floor is quiet at this time of evening. Most of the other business owners have already gone home. Eden walks towards the secret lift, which is reserved for parcels. It's the one time of the day Eden doesn't care about doing the right thing. I wait until the beep of the lift sounds. I take the lift to the ground floor and exit via the main doors, making sure to waft my security pass in front of the guard, who asks to see it every day. The route to the station follows a bend, from which it's possible to see Eden walking ahead and talking on his phone. He's probably telling his partner about how much he hates the job, and how everything will be alright once he gets a better one. Eden's walking fast enough so that no one could catch him without running. He crosses the road without much regard for the oncoming traffic, which means he gets a head start on me. He wants to get home as fast as he can. He doesn't want to dawdle or look at the view, which consists of a motorway under-pass and hedgerows with cigarette butts. There's a grey apartment block that's considered retro and cool in the eyes of people who don't have to live there. Stella Artois, which was once called Milton Keynes, doesn't have a centre. There's a central commerce district, but it feels more like the central square in a grid than the pinnacle of anything. It's just the same as all the other squares, except for the flat-box train station and the large Mecca Bingo. Its ugliness has its own determined beauty. It makes no concessions to anyone. The purpose of the exercise is to watch Eden from afar, and see how close I can get. He's fortunate that I'm very unfit. If it were possible, I'd follow him all the way home and observe him from the garden window. I'd watch him sitting at the kitchen table while his partner — a sexual health nurse — starts an argument about money. The lack of money is nothing compared with his lack of purpose. I turn the corner and witness a surge of office workers emerging from the station. Hundreds of people criss-cross and manage to avoid contact like well-behaved atoms. Eden doesn't want to push, but he's forced to. It's the only way of getting past. It's possible, with some persistence, to find a way through. There are enough polite people to make it possible. The queue makes it look as if there's something exciting to wait for, but it's just a train ticket barrier. I wrestle through the crowd. Through all this, it's possible to see Eden, who swipes his season ticket against the scanner, proceeds through the barrier and consults his phone, no doubt for job ads or angry text messages. The speed at which Eden walks almost suggests he knows I'm coming. This is the point at

which we lose contact, and I can no longer
see what I want to see. That's the end of it. I
won't be able to reach him. He'll be in a
rush to catch the 18.56 to Vodafone.

4

BEHAVIOURAL FRAMEWORK

We refer to it as *the bribe*. The regular knees-up where we make them feel valued, so long as they don't ask for better working conditions; and so long as they upload pictures on social media so that everyone thinks we're a fun company. It's an integral part of our brand-building strategy. After all, you can't share an image of an insecure job, but you can show the world that you work for Lingua Franca, who put money behind the bar and will lend you all the confetti you need. On Halloween we give them apples to bob. On Valentine's we give them scissors and glue to make heart-shaped cards. At Christmas we take them for dinner and attendance is compulsory. We present it as a reward, which isn't wrong exactly. They like getting drunk.

The pub is located at the bottom of our building. The customers include office workers and tired, drunk men who sit at the bar all day. The lighting is bad and not in a soft, candlelit way. No one has taken the initiative to draw the curtains. I have nothing to do with ordering drinks — that task belongs to Nigel. I lean on his shoulder and whisper the pin number: 1985. My involvement extends to buying alcohol for everyone. It means I can opt out when it comes to any social interaction. My strategy is to hover, which gives me the choice on whether I want to escape. There is a corner section, which Nigel reserves every time. There are people trying to get my attention from either direction. Some of them tug at my sleeve and some of them tap my shoulder. Everyone says things like 'Sit with us, Miles!' A couple of them shuffle along to make room at the table. I sit next to Eden.

It's Eden who starts the conversation. 'You alright, mate?' I tell him I'm alright. 'Good week for sales,' he says. He mentions the problem of updating the sales report, which has been locked for editing. I wonder if Eden really wants to have this discussion. He's twenty-odd, but he looks much older. He's got close-cropped hair and blue-toned bags under his eyes. He looks in need of a spa detox. Someone should straighten his back and de-clog his pores. Much of his chat relates to work and how he should have closed a deal for Wigan or Scunthorpe.

I tell him, 'It's alright, mate. You've worked

hard. You're a high-quality individual. And that's what we need at Lingua Franca.' He gives a solemn nod. 'As far as you're concerned, the sky's the limit. Office manager . . . head of sales . . . ' He appears to lose concentration. It's as though I've flicked a switch and turned him off.

'Excuse me,' he says. Eden gets up and walks through the double doors.

The rest of the group cheer as Nigel puts a tray of pint glasses on the table. They're glad to receive the drinks; they're lost desert explorers in receipt of water. There are two distinct tribes: the graduates and the sales team. The former exist in a permanent state of disappointment. Their academic selves had imagined a different future, a world where ideas were important and young people could make a difference. They assumed they would exist like characters in their favourite books and films. They arrived in an office job and wondered whatever happened. The sales team has different expectations. They drink beer rather than wine and they'd rather visit Benidorm than Brixton. They've already glimpsed an alternative world. They've worked in shops, gyms, supermarkets, pubs, catering halls, kitchens and call centres. In light of this, they're delighted to work for Lingua Franca. They're amazed they're able

40

to wear a suit, or look at their name on an entry pass. Unlike the graduates, the sales team never had a dream to begin with. What unites each tribe is that they like being drunk. They like being drunk more than they like drinking. As a group, almost all the chat concerns work. They talk about how they'd do things differently, if only they were in charge. It moves onto a discussion about who should date whom, and who'd make the prettiest couple. Even if some of them laugh, they're secretly keen to hear the verdict. It descends into a bout of in-jokes, a competition to see who can tell the best stories. No one is very good at listening. Nigel serves no purpose in this context other than to keep a lid on any chaos. He will permit the group to go wild, provided there are predefined terms which stipulate what exactly is meant by wild. Good, clean fun and all that. My plan — to dissolve into silence — is executed well. The only threat comes from the drunk barstool men who try to make conversation with the women in our team. When no response is offered, the men start swearing for no apparent reason. One of them makes an obscene gesture. Nigel is watching without saying anything. And in any case, he would make the feeblest of security guards. He looks in my direction to see if I'm safe. One of the posh hedgehog graduates tries to raise an objection with the drunks; they squabble for a moment and come to an understanding that the hedgehog should just accept the abuse. Finally, the men find someone else to harass.

I tell Nigel I'm going. He's reluctant to let me walk alone, but lacks the authority to tell me what to do. Nigel clinks a glass and the rest of the team fall silent. 'Ladies and gentlemen, may I have your attention please?' Nigel thinks he should talk like this because he's second-in-command and second-in-command beats all the rest. 'Let me draw your attention to Miles, who would like to say a few words. Come on, Miles. Give us a speech.'

They all bang the tables and chant, 'Speech, speech, speech!' The vibe is friendly rather than a desire to see me fail. 'Umm . . . thanks, everyone.' My job is to focus their minds on what's important: drink, money, survival. I have little to say, which means I raise a glass and propose a toast. I address them as individuals as best I can. I praise the sales team for their efforts in promoting Lingua Franca. I congratulate the web designers, coders, marketers and admin bods. We have a brilliant team, I remind them. We will travel to Barrow-in-Furness and create a spectacle for which Lingua Franca is renowned. 'Let's remember why we're here — yes, to recast the English language and make our mark on history. But friends, we're also helping to change the direction of travel in towns up and down the country. Ask Doncaster. Ask Waterstones. At a time when local budgets are being slashed, we're the ones giving towns a new lease of life: a foundation, a future. We're proud that we make a profit, but proud, too, of our ability to make a massive impact.' They applaud. They look at me as the favoured one, the cool art teacher to Nigel's deputy head. 'Don't forget, you're history makers. When someone compiles a history of the English language, there'll be a chapter marked Lingua Franca.' I'm speaking to an audience of drunks. They're at their most supportive but least capable of comprehending the words. 'So, let us raise our glasses . . . to us!'

★　★　★

The beauty of the compound is that you can imprison yourself easily. If anyone were to force entry, they could only proceed were they to make lots of noise. Ptolemy's eyes widen, which means that someone's approaching from the gravel path. She's ready to pounce on my behalf. The good thing about

Darren is that he's always on time. I could ring for Darren at four in the morning and he'd come along. The security industry has an unintended egalitarian trait — taking kids from the streets and giving them a job. They employ kids like Darren and tell them it's a good thing to be a tough bastard. Darren's firm offers to protect high-risk clients: Quran defacers and tabloid witch hunt victims. I'm one of their most reliable customers. There was a period following the renaming of Stoke-on-Trent that Darren became a permanent guard-in-residence at the compound. The alert level has since been downgraded, but only a little. There is no dignity in having to leave the house with a security guard. It would be nice to walk alone, if the risks weren't so great. Even now, eighteen months since Milton Keynes became Stella Artois, many of the townspeople would like to make my life as difficult as possible. The charge is that I've degraded language and undermined what it means to belong to a community. They ask me rhetorical questions like *where does it end?* I tell them there doesn't need to be an end. This is only the beginning.

Darren doesn't look well. His eyes tell me this. It's not something he'd admit to, even if it were obvious. He needs to pretend he's strong enough to cope with anything. 'Good

44

morning, sir.' He doesn't really mean it when he smiles. He probably gets advice from his mum. She'll say, 'Whatever you do, just tell him he's brilliant.' He's been told what to do for so long that he can barely remember how to think. He soaks things up. 'Shall we go straight to the office this morning?' I nod. There's no danger as we walk, and it's not certain what Darren could do even if there was. He's a deterrent. He could be capable of anything, or nothing at all.

The neighbourhood is a mixture of clean and dirty money: doctors and drug dealers, rich pimps and hedge fund managers. There's always construction work happening, a constant drilling and the sound of wood being thrown into a skip. Every so often you see a white van patrolling the street — the remit is to identify non-residents and tell them to leave. Behind the railings, the trees are so high you can barely see the houses. The street names reflect a pastoral past, which in a modern context, feels like some sort of joke. Lambton Avenue means 'the town where lambs are sold'. Nothing like this happens anymore.

Darren looks through a gate. 'Some big arse houses, man.' Darren lives with his mum in a modest block of council housing surrounded by metal bins on wheels. We exit through a gate and enter the real world, where roads are public, not private, and people don't stop you from looking at their house. I mention the previous night, and how everyone got drunk. Darren does a good job of disguising his disappointment he wasn't invited. The further we walk the more it seems like we have nothing to say. For Darren, it's an exercise in walking the dog. I should bark when I want to go home.

'I don't know, Darren. Sometimes I think I should be doing more with my life. Do you ever get that?'

'No, sir.'

'If there was an asteroid that destroyed everything on earth, what would I have achieved?' Darren's too afraid to speak. 'Can I tell you a secret, Darren?' I don't want to hear his response. I'm telling him a secret. 'I'm a slow reader. I used to teach English, but I read none of the books. I taught a whole course using SparkNotes. I'm good at collecting books, but not so much reading them. You should see my shelf. Kendal says — '

'Raaa!' Darren says, pointing at a hubcap on the kerb. He looks at the hubcap, which has no novelty, other than the fact it's fallen from a wheel. The normal order of planetary events has been disturbed. Then Darren seems to realise he's gone off-script — the script being to listen to whatever comes out of my mouth.

'But you know . . . maybe it doesn't matter that I don't read. It's good to be a charlatan. Being a charlatan takes talent.'

'Yes, sir.'

'I like to read *about* books, though. I could tell you lots of different opinions on the Bible, but I never want to read the Bible itself.'

'The Bible's boring, man.'

'*Exactly.*' I put a stress on *exactly* only because I want Darren to say something. 'Sure, it would nice to read more. But it's not like anyone at work's gonna test me on *Anna Karenina*. I'm a qualified . . . language creator.'

The conversation runs aground. We've talked for as long as needed. We walk past the old house where Kendal and I were supposed to live, and where she still does. It's an Edwardian house, somehow still intact despite the wrecking ball damage all around us. She hasn't bothered to mow the front lawn in months; the grass is wild and uneven, with a wheelbarrow almost hidden from view. She needs to do something about the broken guttering. At the gate is the problem tree. It needs a tree surgeon to trim the roots, or the house will fall over. She's done nothing about the tree.

We walk a little further, under the motorway, and emerge outside the office.

'Do you need to go anywhere else, sir?'

'No, I'm fine from here.'

'You never know who's out there, you know.'

'Thanks.'

There is an order in which Darren's supposed to ask me things. One of the questions is meant to be 'Have you had a good afternoon?' which will probably come soon. He squints as if he's trying to remember something. 'Have you had a good afternoon?'

'Yes, Darren.'

He walks me as far as the fob entrance. With no advance warning, Kendal walks towards us with four bags of shopping. She has no freedom of her hands; she's weighed down like an unbalanced pendulum scale. She's unable to prevent the wind blowing her hair back. There is no longer a duty to keep opinions to oneself. She puts on a respectable third-party smile on account of Darren's presence. She looks happy I have company, which means I'm not in imminent danger of being killed.

'Another day of ruining the world?' She

looks at the office tower as if it were something to pity.

'Something like that.'

She nods. She wants me to know she can talk about work, but only if she's allowed to emphasise her disgust. 'We're doing a roast next weekend. You're invited.'

'But they hate me.'

She rents a couple of bedrooms to her teacher friends. It's easy to imagine them sitting in the kitchen at night, discussing how awful I am. I'm not a monster exactly, but our separation has given Kendal's friends the freedom to say whatever they like.

'It's a triple date. I need a partner.'

'Why can't you find one?'

'Because there aren't any fucking men in this town. They're all IT contractors. Bank managers . . . '

Darren spends a moment looking at his shoes. We make no effort to integrate him. Darren's the rope and we're the tug o' warriors.

'You should meet Eden. He's depressed.'

'Who's Eden?'

'He works here. I stalked him the other day.'

'Why?'

'I wanted to see what his life's like.'

'What's it like?'

'Shit.'

She mentions how she once taught an Eden as a teenager. She sees him around sometimes. Cropped hair, grey beard.

'That's the one.'

'He was a poet. Or at least he wanted to be.'

'Well, he works in telesales now.'

She likes to stay in touch with her pupils. They're no longer pupils but she still thinks of them as such. 'Give him my love.' It's a shame that Kendal should have any connection to our workplace. She doesn't need to know what we're up to. All she's meant to know is that we're making money and we're able to live as a consequence. That's what we do. It's to Darren's credit that he's able to stand and listen. He exists on the margins, always there but never belonging. Kendal lifts her shopping and smiles at Darren. 'Keep him safe, will you?'

'Yes . . . lady.'

He avoids eye contact, doing the routine of a Buckingham Palace guard. He probably wanted to say *Mrs Platting*. He lacked the conviction. Kendal says she will call me about the roast. She waves as if I were standing far away. There's no kiss on the cheek, which is a shame, and something to reflect upon.

★ ★ ★

It's not a day in which anyone can do much work. It's a day in which bodies are allowed to recover and minds allowed to rest. Everyone seems to be in a general state of disrepair. Some of them have trouble clearing their throat. No one seems to have washed. It's not just the effects of alcohol — it's the unrequited love, unanswered text messages, cheating on partners and all the things that account for the spike in internal email traffic. I hang my coat on the hook. There's a general understanding that I'm the only one who's allowed to be late. Straight away there's a queue of young graduates, who smile for my attention like I'm a waiter who hasn't brought the bill. I look at my mobile as I walk — an excuse to avoid their gaze. I get halfway across the room.

'Miles, can I ask you about the logo?' The graduates tend to ask lots of questions. They prefer problems to solutions.

The next one says, 'When you've spoken to Karen, have you a got a moment to look over the press release?'

Someone else says, 'When you've spoken to Ed, can you check the voiceover?'

I raise a hand and signal *no more questions*. My method of leading by example

51

is to avoid leading anything. 'I'm happy for you guys to deal with it.'

They all seem to shrink at once. If they say anything, it's a simple 'of course'. It takes a while for things to regain their usual rhythm. The tech team monitor social media for any attempts to kill us. The digital marketers analyse online traffic as a means of gauging excitement. The graphic designers sit in a circle and discuss the brand values of Barrow-in-Furness. Most of the noise comes from the telesales desk. They're talking to Cleethorpes, Bognor Regis and Westgate-on-Sea. Their objective is to overcome resistance.

'Forgive me, sir, but are you honestly saying you want to leave two hundred grand on the table just for the sake of tradition?' Eden lets out a laugh. 'I mean, fine — if that's financially viable. But what would your constituents say?' There's much to admire in Eden's work. He combines the graduate outlook with real-world schtick. His patter is better than anyone else's. 'Okay, sir . . . yes, no problem, sir. I've been called a lot worse, sir . . . ' He always puts down the phone in the loudest way possible. 'That was a train wreck.'

'It sounded good, mate. Who was it?'

'Lincoln.'

'Lincoln? That's not a shithole. Don't be so hard on yourself.'

We're in a race to sign up a honeypot town, somewhere with a castle or cathedral. There are 48,083 UK cities, towns and villages. On the wall is a table with thousands of UK settlements ranked according to average income, number of graduates, job prospects, house prices and such. We index the towns using a colour code: the golden towns are the likes of Cambridge, Bath and Oxford, none of which will take our calls. Then we have the yellow tier, the minor posh towns that lack brand value, the Winchesters and Cheltenhams. Then it's the beige: Reading, Colchester, Maidstone, Northampton. Finally, the bottom of the table is where most of our activity is focused — towns with low employment and low visitor numbers: Cumbernauld, Canvey Island, Barrow-in-Furness. The brands, of course, are limitless. Our partnerships team engage with businesses, take them to lunch and persuade them of the benefits of town branding. We have 150 companies waiting to bid for each town's naming rights. The towns sign up on the proviso we can pair them with a suitable (and lucrative) naming rights partner. Following a sale, our partnerships team advise the town on which naming rights partner would resonate with their constituents. We might suggest that affluent Edinburgh be renamed after a chic wool company, or that progressive Bristol call itself Planet Organic. When the bidding commences, the naming rights for somewhere like Ipswich might fetch a couple of million a year, but an Oxford or a Cambridge would attract hundreds of millions. I present myself to the room as open-to-business. 'Listen up, guys. I want to see more historic towns. More spires, yeah? Eden's done a great job hammering Lincoln. If you sign up a top-twenty town, I'll buy you a holiday to Las Vegas. Then you can sign up Las Vegas.'

In tandem they consult their computer databases, lift their receivers and whisper with one another about who's got Windsor and who's got York. Eden photocopies something — a completed direct debit form — which he likes to keep in a drawer. He's organised, even when it comes to things that don't affect his ability to make a sale. Eden puts the form on his desk. He stares at me and says he's going for a smoke. He slings a coat over his shoulder and leaves.

Without Eden, they often lose focus. I look at the team and clap my hands. 'Give it twenty minutes and you can all have a fag break.' I feel comfortable leaving the room in the knowledge that we have something resembling a business. I enter the side office where Nigel is on the telephone.

'Yes . . . we've got toilet roll. We just need six outdoor toilets. How long will it take to install?'

There's a sheet on his desk that lists things like *detergent* and *beer*. On the computer screen is a map of Barrow-in-Furness. Nigel's remit is to arrange the construction of our unit base, the scheduling of events, and to ensure we pay no tax on anything whatsoever. Nigel puts down the phone at last. He hasn't touched his sausage sandwich. He leans back and sighs, giving the impression he hates his job, when really he'd have nothing better to do. He runs through the list. 'We've got the portable toilets, one table tennis table, one mini-fridge, one big-fridge . . . '

'What's the weather like?'

'Cold. I've ordered some outdoor heaters.' Nigel leans back and makes a noise of mock exasperation. 'So much to do!'

'What about security?'

'We should put a bounty on the head of your eventual killer. What do we think — two million?'

'Just get a couple of guards.'

'You can bring Darren.'

'Fine.'

Nigel has small eyes and a patchy

undergrowth beard. He looks like someone who spent his entire university life in a darkened room playing *World of Warcraft*. He looks over his notes and tries to recollect something about train platforms. 'By the way, they want to ambush you.'

'Bring some batons, then.' History tells us that planning is essential. We've learnt from our mistakes. At the naming ceremony, we no longer serve scotch eggs — they're good missiles. We've learnt how to pronounce *Clitheroe*.

We notice some of the graduates pawing at the window, somewhat distressed, as if they were trapped in a sinking ship. The door swings open and we're told to come and look. Everyone now seems to be gathered at the window, staring at something. It seems that all the activity has stopped. The telephone is ringing and no one seems to notice. The focus is on the roof opposite, where someone is crouched at the edge like a cautious swimmer thinking about whether to plunge. I've bitten my lower lip but I don't feel the sensation. Is it really Eden? Is it just an Eden lookalike who's going to fix the air chiller? It doesn't seem likely. Engineers don't wear chequered shirts. We don't need binoculars to see that it's Eden. He looks like he belongs on the roof. He doesn't care that we're just opposite, with our hands pressed against the glass. He looks focused. He doesn't seem to notice our waving hands; we're a football terrace trying to distract the penalty taker. To Eden, we must look like the ones who need help.

'Nigel?'

Nigel doesn't have a protocol. There's no precedent, which means he's got nothing to refer to in the brand catalogue. He walks in between the onlookers, making a quiet, strange suggestion that everyone should disperse. He says, 'Nothing to see, ladies and gents,' but he doesn't get a response. There's plenty to see. No one from street level seems to know what's happening. There are people entering and exiting the train station. The pigeons watch from the roof opposite.

I want to believe Eden's looking at me, even when he's looking straight ahead. Only he can understand what's happening. He seems relaxed. He just wanted to go outside for a smoke. He happened to find the emergency stairwell. That's all that's happened. He rises to his feet. He appears to size up the space in front of him. He breathes out and causes us to brace.

'Eden . . . '

He looks at us — all of us. He closes his eyes. Some of the women begin to scream.

The lads wave their arms and shout. He darts into a sprint and leaps mid-air into the only thing he's sure about, the only thing that's certain.

5

BRAND REPOSITIONING

They've not given me enough paper. On the floor are the strewn sheets with everything I've written. The doctor passes one of the sheets to the nurse, who passes it to the psychiatrist. Everyone's reading my story. I focus my pen on the only remaining white space.

Get me some paper.

The nurse breaks out into dimples. The grey squirrel nods. They're happy that I'm playing the game.

In the absence of something to write on, I can only use my voice. '*Vamos!*' They seem to be panicked by this. The nurse rushes to the drawer and looks inside. She returns with some clean paper. I rouse myself into a sitting position. The nurse puts a pillow behind my back. She pulls down the retractable TV screen and makes sure I know how to turn it on, and where I can access the silent films. She grabs a pen from the desk and writes:

You're doing very well.

She does everything with a smile. She endorses every aspect of my being, so long as I say nothing. The cleaner takes my cup. The physiotherapist rubs the sole of my foot. All I need is a gold star. I seem to command most of the attention. The bell rings from another bed and the nurse ignores it. The bay has six different beds, all occupied by males. I'm reminded of the times I've been brought together with strangers, like my freshers week a long time ago at Southampton University — now The Wagamama Institute. The patients seem to be half asleep. One of them has a foot suspended in a cast. Every now and then someone makes a groan. It's hard to tell whether they're deteriorating or just can't be bothered anymore. It's as though I'm the only one who's alive.

A trolley comes and the caterer puts down a tray — mashed potato and a metal cylinder of vegetables. She presents a menu with different dessert options. I point at the BlackBerry tart, formerly Bakewell tart. I write a note:

Mustard, please.

The caterer turns to her colleague and makes the letter 'M' with her middle three fingers.

The message is understood. I peel the cellophane wrapper from my plastic tub of gravy. On the TV screen is a weather report. I put on my headphones and realise it makes no difference because everything's been muted. The weatherman is talking aloud but the words are subtitled. He points to South West England, to Allianz, where temperatures will drop to within nine degrees celsius. In Pfizer, Surrey, there's every chance of rain. The Environment Agency has issued a warning about driving conditions in Cath Kidston. The nurse adjusts the room temperature. I raise a thumb. In the corner of my eye, the grey squirrel accompanies a patient into the corridor. I remove the headphones and put the tray on the side. I swivel into a sitting position and pull the slippers onto my feet. The nurse seems to watch.

Where are you going?

I make my first attempt at sign language by pointing to my crotch. She corrects me: you're supposed to do a double-tap of the shoulder blade with your index finger. Next time I'll know.

If you're looking for Kendal, you won't find her.

Why?

It's a big hospital.

Where is she?

The nurse makes an exaggerated shrug. She passes my note to the physiotherapist, who does the same thing. It would make sense to indulge the game and see where it gets me.

I was hoping she'd be here.

You can see her when you've recovered.

But I'm fine.

The nurse leans down to remove a can of Heineken from the trolley. She puts it on my bedside table. I've never met a nurse who encourages bedside drinking.

Aren't you going to tell me what happened next?

She looks at me with the expectation that whatever I write is going to be amazing. She wants to know the rest of the story. I'm made to feel like I'm cute. I'm interesting. I tell great stories with my pen and it's not what I write that's brilliant so much as the way that I tell it. I should just write as much as I can, and speak aloud when I can't find the words. I'll write about Kendal, and Nigel, and all the others. All I need is a can of Heineken — the beer, not the place in West Yorkshire.

★   ★   ★

In the moments after Eden falls, Nigel gives a creditable performance. He writes an email to all members of staff, emphasising the need to remain cautious. For some reason, he states that Eden would never do something so stupid as to take his own life. It must have been an accident. When it comes to phoning the police, and recording what we'd seen in writing, Nigel makes a point of working until the necessary duties have been done. This is Nigel's preferred state of affairs. He likes everything to be a procedure. He wouldn't mind if every day was a crisis.

Nigel finds me in the side office. 'He left this on his desk. I've made a photocopy. I'll give the original to the police.' Nigel puts it in front of me. It's a completed direct debit form signed by Eden. On the other side is a handwritten note. 'I don't think you want to read it, mate. It's not all bad. But he's not our biggest fan, put it that way.'

I stare at the letter without taking in the words. I fold the letter and put it inside my jacket. 'Another time.'

Through the glass we can see the office as we've never seen it before: idle and silent. They seem to be facing one another, consumed for once in each other's company. The sales targets on the board might as well belong to another age. Nothing seems important except to love and support one another. In our own little cell, we mimic their silence. We sit and say nothing. Nigel lacks the humanity to construct sentences that feel appropriate for the moment. 'Puts a spanner in the works for Barrow, doesn't it?' I look at Nigel as though he were deserving of pity. He seems to take note of this. 'I'm just saying.' We look at the room opposite. There's nothing in the rulebook, no guide to consult. 'They'll expect you to say something, mate.'

'I know.'

Nigel never says 'mate'. In a normal situation, it would sound wrong coming from Nigel. In the context of Eden's passing, it feels warm and sincere. It was the right thing to say. I let Nigel put an arm around my shoulder. Then we step aside and make sure we don't make eye contact.

On each desk, they make an effort to swivel their chair and look towards me. Everyone wants a distraction. They look at me like the President of the United fucking States. They're the press assembly, waiting for my verdict. I approach what amounts to the lectern — the desk behind which I can stand and begin my address.

'Afternoon, folks.'

It's rare that the whole office listens to me at the same time. They can see I'm having difficulty in my attempts to smile.

'I know that many of you witnessed what happened earlier. We've since spoken to the police . . . ' It's a manageable situation until I get closer to the actual subject. My voice begins to tremble. I feel compelled to put my hand in my pocket. 'I'm sorry to confirm that Eden Darby, our colleague and friend, has passed away.' *Passed away* is the right term. You shouldn't announce that someone's dead. I make a conscious effort to stop my eyes from watering. If I were to cry, it would break their faith in everything. This is the moment. It only seems real at this particular moment. I can feel Nigel's hand against my back. Most of them ditch the professional conceit — they permit themselves to break down. They sob into their hands and hold one another. The emotion has wrought its damage. Almost everyone has blotched skin. 'We've been hit by a tragedy this afternoon. I want you all to go home. An announcement about the Barrow project will be made in the coming days. It goes without saying that Eden will always be in our thoughts.' There's no official cue for the silence. It just happens because people want it to. It feels better that nothing is said.

Everything seems to intensify. On my mobile phone I have five missed calls from Kendal. The press team puts out a statement, which pays tribute to Eden. The web manager transfers our files to a back-up server in the event our building were hit by a mortar bomb. Nigel answers his mobile phone, and tells a journalist we won't make a further statement. The main objective concerns exiting the building, and how this might be achieved. From the window we can see what awaits us: a press assembly. A real one. And news cameras. I consider making a joke about how popular we are, but think better of it. Nigel pulls on a fluorescent yellow bib and tells everyone to form a queue in the corridor. Half the team are told to evacuate via the stairs, the other half via the back elevator. 'This is not a drill!' Nigel says. No one seems to know what it is.

We're the last ones to leave. We walk through the underground car park and exit through the security gate, showing our passes to the guard. Darren is there. He opens the back doors to a white transit van. He asks if I've had a good day, then corrects himself with 'sorry, sorry'. His conversational template has let him down. Nigel and I sit cross-legged in the back of the van. Darren drives. We manage to travel into the centre of Stella Artois, through the press scrum. I know the cameras are there, and I know what's coming next. Still, I turn to face them just in time for the flash. I'm sure they have a good shot. I'm sure they'll have a headline ready, a story to run. I'm making a getaway, a cardboard cut-out villain. Cut me out and stick me on the tabloid. Press down with glue. Turn the page.

* * *

We make time to mourn, which involves suspending work, speaking to no one, lots of sleep and the unwelcome realisation that I don't have a life outside of my job. I make unnecessary appointments with an electrician and a bathroom fitter. The bathroom's fine, but it would be good to know this for certain. The spotlights in my living room need to be replaced. I decide my new life mission is to replace the spotlights. I get a replacement bulb from the drawer. I pull out a chair and set about tapping the spotlight, loosening the metal spring. Then I pull it out, letting the wire dangle. Ptolemy rubs against the chair. In times like this, Ptolemy is more of a nuisance than something to cherish. She makes out that she needs to eat, when really she's forgotten there's a bowl upstairs. My mobile rings. The only thing more important than fixing the spotlight is to answer the phone.

In my brief telephone call with the Barrow officials, we come to an understanding that we should rearrange the launch. Barrow will be Barrow for another week. The councillor offers his condolences and we agree it's a tragedy that could have struck any company.

Later that day I get a call from Kendal, who wants to know if I've heard the news. 'Twenty-three, Miles! He was twenty-three.'

'I know.'

'It's all I can fucking think about. Do you know what he said to me in year ten? He said I was his favourite teacher. Isn't that nice?'

'That's nice.'

'He was twenty-three, Miles.'

'I know.'

She describes what I already know — that Eden jumped from the roof, and that no one could see it coming. She says that Lingua Franca should make a contribution to the

68

funeral costs and I find myself nodding. I say a few words about Eden. He was a credit to the company. It seems like anything I say is a cause for irritation. I'm losing the contest for who liked Eden the best.

'I don't think you should feel guilty,' Kendal says.

'I don't feel guilty.'

'You weren't to know.'

'Know what?'

'That he was suicidal working for you.'

* * *

We meet that afternoon at a small dirty café. It's an occasion that necessitates the presence of Darren, who sits outside with a cigarette and a copy of *The Sun*.

'Doesn't he want to come inside?'

'He's fine out there.'

Kendal looks like she hasn't slept. In the silence, the café seems louder than it should. Every clink of a glass seems to matter. 'The Lord builds up Jerusalem. He heals the broken-hearted, and binds up their wounds.' She rubs her eyes with the small, insufficient piece of tissue that came with our bacon bap. 'I promised myself I wouldn't cry.'

'That's what I'm here for.'

She holds my arm. Were it not for the

69

annoyingly tight seating, we would hug properly. She presses her face onto my arm. There's snot on my sleeve. A part of me wonders whether she brought me here so that I'd have to show emotion in front of builders.

'I'm making a speech at the funeral,' she says. 'I thought you should know.'

'That's nice.'

'You don't know what I'm going to say yet.'

I look at her with my best *don't you dare* face.

'I won't mention you.'

'Good.'

'I'll mention what you represent.' I frown as hard as I can. This is the best way of registering my anger. 'Don't look at me like you're constipated,' she says. 'Something like Eden was waiting to happen. You think you can hide in your fortress and never think about anybody. Well, you know what? There's a world out there and you're responsible to it.'

She's quoting something, but I don't know what. It's how she gets the upper hand. It's how we used to argue.

'You're right.'

'Yes!' She punches the air and looks around, deciding whether it's the time or place to do a victory dance.

I want to make a confession. 'He wrote to

me. I'm in the letter.'

She looks at me like I've said something offensive. 'Whose letter?'

I stare.

'What did he say?'

'I haven't read it yet.'

'Repent, then, and turn to God, so that your sins be wiped out!' Kendal lifts her arms and laughs. Despite being an atheist, she has an obsession with religious proverbs. She sees the beauty in it. 'You've got to read it, Miles.' She's got hold of something. She's onto it. 'You can change. You can repent!'

I put my hand inside my coat pocket. I can feel Eden's letter. I decide, on this occasion, to do nothing. 'Shall we get the bill?'

Kendal flings her arms upwards. 'Fine.' She brushes my shoulder to remove a fleck of something. She frowns at my badly knotted tie. I remind Kendal that she doesn't need to think about this stuff anymore. 'You can't look like shit though,' she says. 'People might think we're still together.' She's trying to remember if there's something to be angry about. 'Are you coming round on Friday? Please say you're coming. I need a date.'

'I'll come.'

'It's the worst idea I've ever had.'

'How romantic.'

'If you're lucky I'll pay for your taxi home.'
'I haven't missed you.'

* * *

We walk down Midsummer Boulevard, which is like a never-ending car park. There are too many open spaces in Stella Artois. I want to feel hemmed in. I want the blind corporate reassurance of tall buildings. Darren walks alongside us. I tell him it would be nice to be left alone. He doesn't detect the signal until I place a twenty-pound note in his palm.

A lady dressed in a ski suit and earmuffs passes us a leaflet. 'Ice skating, guys?' I look at Kendal, who lifts her arm so that I might take it — a mock-courtly love sort of thing. We're going ice skating.

I slip on my boots and walk along the rubber, losing my balance as the blade gets caught in the groove. Kendal laughs and I give her a look that says *like you're any better!* She sticks out a tongue and starts to walk, more elegantly than me, as it turns out. We lock arms again.

'Look at the ice, you idiot!' She bends her knees to demonstrate the best position. 'You've got to bend your knees and glide. You're not gliding. You're stuck in the mud.' I grasp for the rail. A couple of children skate past. Is there anyone worse than me? I look around but there's no one worse. 'Come on.' She takes my hand and we become a duo. I manage to balance a little. I move my legs like a lamb learning to walk. We walk to the middle of the rink. Behind the barrier a crowd of mulled-wine drinkers are beginning to watch. We're the object of their gaze, the thing to notice. Some of the children look at us. Kendal holds my hand while she does a twirl. 'Now you try.' I feel myself wobble. I start to move my legs and she lets me free. I begin to totter, flailing my arms like a mad swinging drunk. My foot begins to slip and suddenly I'm falling; all I can think is to clench my fists. I land hard on my right shoulder. It's only when I limber up into a sitting position and lay out my legs that I can see Kendal laughing. She lifts me to my feet and ruffles the ice from my hair. 'Come on, Bambi. Let's get you some stabilisers.'

We take an early exit and walk to the mulled wine. One of the kids gives me a high five.

6

EXPRESSION SESSION

We stand with the mourners, circled around the entrance. Most people seem to know each other. No one has any inhibition about sobbing in the company of friends. Some have assigned themselves the role of giving hugs; others need to be held. No one cares if they're being watched. No one is required to control their emotion. It's all there. The arrival of the coffin brings us all together. Someone approaches the hearse and opens the passenger doors. Eden's family emerge. Everyone steps out of their way.

The coffin is carried into the church. It's not a building that inspires awe. The only reason you know it's a church is the fact that it has a cross on the front. Otherwise it could be a school gym. It doesn't feel like you need to wipe your feet before entering. The church must have been chosen by Eden's parents, who want to remind us that Eden was once a good Christian boy. He wasn't always the Eden we knew at the end. The Eden we actually liked. Everyone smiles at the clergyman, who passes a sales brochure and a pamphlet. The coffin is positioned on a platform in view of the congregation and gallery. I find a position at the back of the room, which will allow an unobstructed escape. If I sit any closer I'd be in the speakers' line of sight. Kendal is sitting a few rows in front but I avoid getting her attention. I don't need a distraction. The event gives us an excuse not to look at one another. Nigel is wearing black gloves, which has the benefit of being good for driving and good for public displays of sadness. By the time Nigel has positioned himself next to me, I've gone through the process of taking it all in. I've thought about what's happening and confronted the event itself — the death. I'm a few seconds ahead of everyone else. The reverend is the first person to speak. He says thank you for coming and asks if everyone can ensure their mobile phones are switched off. One or two people are feeling their pockets for their phone. According to the pamphlet, the first contribution will be made by Eden's father. He emerges from the back of the room. A man with soft white hair that doesn't cover the full length of his scalp. He stands in front of the lectern without making a fuss of anything. There's no applause. To clap would seem inappropriate. He looks at the audience for a moment and smiles to acknowledge their presence.

'I know it's hard,' he begins, 'but the only way we can get through this is to remember Eden as he really was. He was a kind and generous spirit. And a bloody great pain in the arse!' Everyone laughs aloud. Mr Darby has unchained them. He has let some light into the room. 'If we look at Eden's life with an open mind, we can understand what he really meant to us. We can remember him in the most truthful way. And we'll remind ourselves there was no one else quite like him.' He manages to keep himself steady. 'I don't think any of us have accepted what's happened. No matter how hard it is, we need to accept it.' Eden's body will soon belong to the earth, he says. But it doesn't matter. He's still with us. He's positioned himself in our thoughts. He has laid claim to our neural pathways. 'If I have one regret — ladies and gentlemen — it's that Eden would never have imagined the love that we see in this room.' Eden's father is an eloquent speaker; he probably went to one of those private schools where they hold oratory classes. He probably works as a lawyer or a high court judge, not for the sake of money or power, but in the benign, paternalistic sense of using one's influence to help those without any. Mr

Darby makes a reference to Eden's job, which made him tired and ill. It weighed him down. It reduced him to being a foot soldier in someone else's empire. 'When I think of his last few months, I think about a man of great intellect who wasn't able to show it. He knew he could do better.' Mr Darby, a post-war child who *never had it so good*, probably never thought his son would make sales calls for eight hours a day. 'Yes, it was tough for Eden over these last few months. He wasn't especially proud of his work for Lingua Franca, an organisation that seeks to franchise and rename British towns under corporate sponsorship. We used to laugh about it together. But in many ways, Eden's story was about courage and integrity. He knew that his daily life brought little in the way of satisfaction, or even personal reward. But he never got sucked into the system. He made a pact with himself that if he couldn't live the way he wanted — which was to live in the service of the world he loved — then there wasn't much point in living at all. His passing is a lesson in how to live. As Eden might have said himself, to live an authentic life is the only life worth living.'

I should avoid looking at Nigel, who doesn't want to acknowledge what's being said. He doesn't want to accept that we could be guilty of anything. It's like Tony Blair listening to Nelson Mandela's call for peace. He doesn't want to hear it. These are the instances where Nigel's presence is required. Nigel knows the patter better than I do. He takes it upon himself to defend the company at whatever cost. He can make the case for why we're not evil, despite all evidence to the contrary. I'm unable to make this argument, or summon the strength.

Mr Darby asks everyone to rise from their seats and join him at the front. It becomes a spectacle, which involves the entire congregation walking towards the coffin. Some people simply touch it with their hand. Others watch from a distance, and mumble whatever needs to be mumbled. The mourners are as one — they're part of a mass, which assembles itself in silence. There is a table of framed photographs of Eden. I know him more intimately now. I can feel Eden as a presence, someone who's staked a position in my unconscious. He hasn't existed in such a way before. Death brings him closer. Mr Darby announces that anyone who wishes to say a few words about Eden's life is welcome to do so. A woman with a peroxide fringe makes an attempt to begin a speech. She makes a false start — stuttering over her words — and finally admits she can't speak. Someone lets her nuzzle into their shoulder. The silence is interrupted by Kendal, who introduces herself as Eden's old English teacher. She taught Eden in his teenage years and knows all about his qualities. For someone who speaks in front of classes every day, Kendal has difficulty keeping her hands still. She doesn't have the same natural style as Eden's father, but she knows what she wants to say.

'People like Eden reminded me of why I became a teacher. He was kind, generous and sweet.' She addresses the whole of the room when she says what a popular person Eden was. She says you're not supposed to have favourites, but it was difficult with Eden because he inspired love by the way he was. He made her job more straightforward than it would otherwise have been. 'Eden was a natural teacher himself. He shared facts about history, or science, but never in a condescending way. He wanted you to learn something and marvel at the world's beauty. He wanted to enrich your experience of life.' The longer she speaks the more confident she seems. It's like she's suddenly able to recollect things she hadn't cared to remember. She tells a story about how Eden once announced to the class that the dot on top of the letter 'i' is called a *tittle*. The last time Kendal saw Eden was outside a cash machine on the high street. Eden talked about his job. 'It's a real shame that his final months were spent doing stuff he hated.' I manage to look at the floor. I bow my head and keep my hands clasped. Lingua Franca, renowned for its callous business ethic, will never arouse feelings of affection among the mourners. For Nigel, it's just another procedure — something we have to get through. 'Lingua Franca wore him out. He was made to feel that he wasn't worth something. But he was. And while we can't hold his employers directly responsible, we can politely remind them that no man is an island, every man is a piece of the continent.' The applause accounts for the gratitude felt by Eden's family and friends. Kendal spoke well. The church has become a courthouse. We're on trial on suspicion of ruining Eden's life.

'Don't worry,' Nigel whispers. 'No one gets murdered at a funeral.'

We exit to a Bob Dylan song. Kendal slows her pace so that she can join us on the walk. We're not certain whether to link arms or carry on as we are. Outside, we congregate where we started. It's raining, which makes sense. We stand on the wet grass and watch the coffin being carried into the vehicle. None of us speak. The good thing is that no one has acknowledged my presence. They know that

Eden's employer has a lot to answer for, but they don't necessarily know it's me. They're not compelled to look at me and protest my existence. This is a good thing — they wouldn't know what to do with me. I recognise the peroxide-blonde woman who walks towards us.

'You're his boss!' One of her teeth is gold. I can tell by the way she snarls. 'You've got some cheek to come here.' She doesn't wait for a reply. 'You've got some brass neck. Did you not read the letter?'

'I wanted to pay my respects.'

'Yeah? Then go home.' She points in the direction of the cemetery gates. 'Murderer.'

Nigel and Kendal do their best to avoid looking at me. The peroxide blonde woman walks away. Nigel mutters something — the essence being that he objects to the word *murderer*. 'Suppose that was his girlfriend, was it? The sexual health nurse?'

'Nigel. Leave it.'

There's a hand on my back, which belongs to Kendal. I don't want to hang around. I walk towards the gates, exactly as I was told. Kendal follows, but I don't want to talk about anything. I ignore the clergyman at the gate who offers another leaflet. The rain continues to fall. I unbutton my jacket and place it over my head.

'Come on, Miles' is all she can say. She follows, on the working assumption that I'll stop at some point. 'She's just upset. The emotions are raw.' She puts a hand on my shoulder and I politely give it back. 'Are you okay?'

'I just want to walk.'

I keep walking, to the point where Kendal doesn't bother to follow. Darren emerges from the white transit van. I pretend not to notice.

'Mr Miles . . . Miles? Mr Platting?'

I keep going. I owe it to myself to keep going. I walk through the part of Stella Artois where everything's been sponsored by us. The main road is named after a bakery chain and the public square is an IT software developer. The local college is sponsored by a triumvirate of banks. The neighbourhood remains run-down, but with more logos on the buildings. Everything is named after something. The software company are reluctant to be associated with neglect, so they're contributing towards the cost of a new public realm. The coffee shops collect money to replace the paving slabs. Everyone wants to make it a desirable place to live, which will enhance the visitor experience and brand value.

It's probably stupid to be walking unaccompanied by Darren. It only occurs to me that I'm doing something stupid at that moment, when I notice how many drunk, brawling men are slapping car bonnets and shouting in the street. If they hate perfectly reasonable members of the public, it's difficult to imagine what they might feel towards me. It's getting dark, which protects me somewhat. The rain is more concerning than the cold — it makes me want to walk faster. I walk fast enough that I don't have to answer the man who's beginning to shout in my direction. I put my head down and I keep walking, despite the wind and the rain. I keep walking until I can no longer hear them shout at me. I cross the metal barrier between the normal world and my fairytale kingdom, where nothing bad is allowed to happen. I find comfort in the large detached houses and unnecessarily wide roads. I like the fact there are cameras hidden in the lamp posts and security guards on patrol. I want to get inside and put on my pyjamas. I want to lay out Ptolemy's dinner, a depressing act, no matter that it's informed by kindness. I want to close the windows, lock the interior doors and turn on the alarm. The barbed wire and anti-climb paint can do the rest. I want to laugh at something on the television. If a loner laughs in his living room and no one hears, does he make a sound? I have my own philosophical question. In front of me are the headlights of a van. I slow my pace. Someone's standing in the road, but it's hard to see under their umbrella. You can see the rain fizzing past in the lamplight. 'Come on, Dickens. Let's get you home.' Kendal lifts the umbrella and shields me from the rain. Somehow, she's perfectly dry. She lifts out an arm so that I might take it. She walks me down the road, where the last fragments of white picket fence make way for machine-brick and machine-metal. She keeps the umbrella upright. We're not quite alone. Darren's at the wheel of the van, which follows some way behind. At the gate to the compound, she offers her gloved hand.

'Are you alright?'

'I'm alright.'

We're alright. We make eye contact, and both of us seem to decide that's too much. It's too much to look at one another in the eye. So we stop doing that. And we say goodnight.

7

ANTONY AND CLEOPATRA

If I'm ever going to have a breakdown, the pet shop will be the place. It's where I'll drop to the floor and call for Darren. It's hard to walk around without getting in someone's way. Everything has been assembled as though it were attic clutter. It's a world of stacked hamster cages and boring goldfish. There's a smell, which I attribute to the hamster cage — a sawdust smell. The lizards enjoy life under a light bulb. There's a dog in a basket but he's not for sale. The parrot is making a fuss about something. Everything is given a sufficient degree of respect. There are cages in which the gerbils can run around, albeit with little chance of escape. Kendal never once came to the pet shop. She saw it as evidence of my decline. She thinks Ptolemy should be a side-project, not the be-all and end-all.

Darren helps to hoist the cat food bags onto the counter. The man at the till recognises me as the person who buys the same cat food pellets every month. He's a tall skinny man whose T-shirts celebrate bands no one likes anymore: Aerosmith, Meatloaf. His hair is long and uncombed, with a bald crown reflecting the light. It's hard to imagine him in any other context. He belongs in the pet shop. He asks about my cat. I mention that Ptolemy's getting bullied by next door's tabby.

'Put some glasses of water outside. Cats don't like water.' He talks about animals like a mechanic might talk about a faulty car — he's more interested in the process of keeping the animal going. 'Have you got cat insurance yet?'

'No.'

'Good. Waste of money.'

Our conversations are limited in scope, for which I take no responsibility. We haven't yet come to the understanding that we're better off saying nothing. He puts everything into a bag, and it's all very slow. The silence is my chance to talk about non-mechanical things, which might hurry him along.

'I'm going to Barrow-in-Furness next week.'

'Chicken's popular.'

I nod. 'We're going to rename it Birdseye-in-Furness.'

He looks lost. I give him some money in exchange for the cat food pellets. Darren stands in the corner, looking into a goldfish tank. He's getting in the way of customers. I receive each bag at a time and summon Darren, my personal shop assistant. We knock into a birdcage as we exit. I don't like coming to the pet shop. It's definitely where I'll have the breakdown.

★ ★ ★

The University of Stella Artois was established following a merger of University Campus Milton Keynes and the University of Bedfordshire. It doesn't have the credentials of a Cambridge, or a Nickelodeon, but it draws upon a large catchment area, from Swindon to Powerade. It attracts a variety of students — from high achievers destined for university to those learning functional skills. In keeping with the rest of Stella Artois, the vice chancellor and governors had decided to rename the university in accordance with the town's naming rights. There was no legal obligation for them to do so. It was a decision undertaken for reasons of practicality. How, for instance, can you advertise the institution as the University of Milton Keynes when the town itself has been renamed? There's a domino effect, which is deliberate and ingenious. If a town is renamed, the university, schools and libraries feel compelled to join the revolution. This is how it goes.

I knock on the door in the hope that Kendal will answer. I don't like coming to the staff room. They hold me in contempt for the fact I left the profession. Miles Platting, former teacher, traitor to the education world, maker of money and destroyer of worlds. They think my life is more glamorous than it is. I know from Kendal that they ask how Lingua Franca's doing, but always with a bitter edge, and never with any hope that I might be doing well. They imagine a world of perks — free drinks at the bar, chauffeur-driven cars — and they feel worse about themselves. I open the door and I'm met with half smiles. Someone says, 'Y'alright, Miles.' They tend to tolerate my existence based on my relationship to Kendal. She only likes the English Literature teachers, who occupy the furthest desks from the entrance. They have a passion for books and getting drunk. Kendal doesn't disguise her contempt for the rest. She calls the older ones *windbags*, and is convinced some of them are sexual predators, if only she had proof. They're of an age where they don't like to debate things; they're just correct, and you better get used to it. They manage to avoid getting sacked due to their superior knowledge of how the teaching inspectors work. One of them — the warthog who teaches history — offers his condolences regarding the death of Eden. I nod, muttering something about it being a sad time for Lingua Franca. Kendal emerges from the kitchen. She smells of strawberry tea. I remove a bottle of wine from the blue plastic bag. 'You might want to keep it chilled.'

Kendal says thanks and puts it inside the mini-fridge.

I reach into the bag and remove Ptolemy's flea drops. 'Drip these behind her ears.'

'Behind the ears. Got it.'

'Only once.'

One of the friendlier women asks about Ptolemy.

'She's good. But she's fighting the neighbour's cat.'

'Oh no.'

I nod. Kendal looks at me like she's worried I'm ill. 'But other than that, she's good.'

The friendly teacher mentions how she puts bottles of water on her lawn, which deters any cats from intruding. 'Cats don't like water.'

'Indeed.'

The other teachers turn from their desks, ready to speak. Someone talks about their dog. It descends into a conversation about animals. Kendal frowns and tugs at my sleeve. 'Have you got half an hour?'

'Why?'

'I've got my English language class in a second.' She passes me a stapled document titled:

What's in a name? Is Juliet correct when she says a rose by any other name would smell as sweet?

There's a bullet point list of questions for the students to consider.

'How do you fancy a bit of guest speaking?'

'Not today.'

'It will help with their homework.'

The teachers suddenly prove they have vocal chords. 'Go on, Miles!' they say. 'You'll love it!'

I look at Kendal, who does a cartoonish flutter of her eyelashes. 'Pretty please? I'll get Ptolemy a present.'

They look at us like it's the most exciting thing they've ever seen.

'Fine.' I hold out an arm and she pulls me along. 'She needs some catnip.'

★ ★ ★

The university looks more like an airport, fireproofed with glass and metal. It seems to have been designed on the basis that someone needs to be thwarted; someone who's desperate to burn it down. On the walk to the classroom, Kendal describes in detail a number of things we need to do, all of which makes me wonder if I shouldn't have bothered. We need to get a guest pass and we need to photocopy some extra sheets. On the walk, Kendal seems to have developed an instinctive ability to spot any students who aren't wearing lanyards round their neck. She seems obsessed with identifying wrongdoing: noise and loitering, in particular. It confounds my expectation that her job only takes place within classroom hours. Really, she never stops working.

'Where's your lanyard?' she points at one student, who reluctantly puts it on. It seems so anti-Kendal — an unfounded respect for authority. 'If they don't wear it, everything breaks down,' she explains. 'A school is like an organ. If it fails, the body can't function.' She can tell I look surprised. She says, 'You're like the colon, Miles. Full of shit.' I give her a gentle shove. We walk to the counter and sign a form, which enables me to receive a guest pass. I quickly put it on, in case she tells me off.

I follow Kendal into the classroom. Here they are — a class of eighteen-year-olds, in their slogan T-shirts and hoodies. The first thing I notice is that a couple of lads look at one another and snigger. I don't really know what's funny. It might be my hair, which even on a good day has a mad professor quality. It might be my unshaven, unkempt, unimpressive beard. I left the house without knowing I'd be teaching a class of teenagers. There is irrefutable evidence that Kendal is a popular tutor. You can see it in the way the students say hello. She starts by talking about a previous assignment, and how the class need to concentrate better. She laments the fact that half the room don't know what an ellipses is. She introduces the purpose of the next assignment, which is to discuss the meaning of language and why it's important. She says she's delighted to welcome a special guest, a specialist in language, as she politely puts it.

'My opponent this afternoon is Miles Platting, founder of the Lingua Franca naming rights agency.' The debate is an important one, she says. We're here to discuss language and its relationship with human beings. It doesn't appear to be a joke. I'm engaged in a contest. 'Miles will be making the case for town branding as a force for good. Lingua Franca, for those who don't know, is committed to renaming every town in the UK after a corporate sponsor. I'm sure all of you can remember when Listerine was called Loughborough, or when Virgin Media was called Stoke-on-Trent. So please, give a warm Stella Artois welcome to Mr Miles Platting.'

They applaud, some of them in an ironic, excessive way.

'Thank you, Kendal. Thank you, everyone.' I spend a moment thanking the college, mostly so I can think about what to say next.

'Sixty seconds,' Kendal says, putting a sand timer upside down on the table. 'Please make your opening statement.'

I smile out of necessity. I decide to make a go of it. 'Language is of course a fascinating object of study. What we recognise at our company is that language can connect with audiences in ways that little else can.'

'And make lots of money,' Kendal interjects, to laughter.

'Yes, that too. But we all make money. Some of it in more legitimate ways than others. The premise of our company is perfectly legal, that being: how is it right for a town's biggest asset — its name — to remain prohibited from working in the interest of its people?' I mention how I'll be visiting

93

Barrow-in-Furness in the days ahead. 'The people in Barrow want jobs, investment, dignity, self-respect . . . they like tradition, but what use is tradition if there's no money in your pocket, no food on the table?'

'It's not a paradigm I recognise,' Kendal steps in. 'Thirty seconds.'

'There are twenty-five languages that die every year. That's two hundred and fifty every decade.' I point a finger at Kendal. 'Your way of doing things — to do nothing — is already resulting in grievous loss, every year. At Lingua Franca, we believe in managing language, to exert our will upon it, and in doing so, to revitalise towns for generations to come.' I almost forget we're debating in front of a class. It feels like we're arguing in my living room. I'm not allowed to storm off. Dereliction of duty, and all that. 'In conclusion, ladies and gents, we reserve the right to name a town — by consent — whatever we so choose.' I seem to disturb them. I'm dangerous. I'm radioactive. 'Language needs to work for us. We are its master, not its slave.'

'Stop!' Kendal lifts the sand timer and puts it upside down again. She looks at me as if she were conducting a cross-examination. 'I'm sorry my opponent holds the English language in such contempt, but let's take a look at the facts.' She walks in front of my path. 'Why do we communicate? Why do we use words? Why not just grunt?' Some of them laugh. 'It's a serious question.' She allows a silence to enable them to think. 'Language is about self-expression. It's about conveying information. It's about poetry. But it's also about who we are, our history, our home . . . our sense of being alive!' They all seem to listen and nod at the appropriate moments. Kendal's one of them, in her heart. She hates authority and loves people. 'The name of your town means something. It's almost sacred.'

'Thirty seconds,' I mumble.

'Next week my opponent will be visiting a fine town, Barrow-in-Furness. A town built on industry and hard work. With one stroke of a pen, Miles will undo hundreds of years of history and leave a community a few hundred grand better off. But in spirit, at least, they will be much, much poorer. I don't want to live in this kind of world! I don't want to live in a fabric softener.' They laugh, and she sips from her strawberry tea. 'So what's in a name?' She points to the whiteboard. 'Would a rose by any other name smell as sweet?' This is the part of the job she enjoys. Kendal is analytical about everything. She could deconstruct the meaning behind a bowl of cornflakes. She's been given carte blanche to develop a course in her own indomitable way. They study the evolution of language, how language is constructed, contemporary discourse, phonetics, and how language is connected to thought and meaning. 'I'll let you guys decide. But at the very least, the discerning among you will understand that language is precious and at great risk from people like Miles Platting.'

'Stop.' The sand timer has finished.

She pulls up a chair and sits on the table, closer to the students. She wafts a hand in my direction. 'The floor is yours.'

I take the opportunity to pace around the room. I begin my own cross-examination. 'I also agree that language matters, but so does progress.' This is a good way to start. 'Progress isn't just about freedom of expression. There are hundreds of towns across this country where people can say whatever they like, but what voice do they really have?' Almost by accident, I seem to have said something worth listening to. They're silent for once. 'And there's a moral point here.' I raise a moral finger. 'Do you want local services? Care in the community? Do you want your rubbish picked up from your street? Libraries. Health visitors. Childcare. These are the things that matter. And sadly, they're not free.' I'm encouraged by the silence. There's an opening. I'm through on goal, with only the keeper to beat. 'Do you want to live in a town that's miserable, dirty and bankrupt, just so you can cling to some old romantic notion? Or do you want to live in a town that's prosperous, vibrant, fun. Wi-Fi enabled! As I said earlier, we own language. It doesn't own us. And naming rights is nothing new. We're not doing anything the Romans weren't doing when they called it Londinium.'

They seem . . . numb. No one knows what to say. And not because they disagree. Just because some things are too awful to agree with.

'Rubbish,' Kendal says.

'Is it?'

'Yes!'

Some of the class also shout 'yes'. This is their escape. A reason to believe there's more to life than what cynical Miles Platting says. Kendal offers them a dream. If you could sell *that*, it would be bigger than Burger King.

'Why should we rename our towns after biscuits or washing powder?'

'If I paid you enough money, would you change your name?'

'No.'

'So, let's say I offer you a million quid to

97

call yourself the name of a biscuit. Would you do it?'

'I've already got a name.'

'But now I'm calling you Wagon Wheel, and everyone has to call you that. But you get a million quid. Are you seriously telling me you'd turn it down?'

'You can call me Hobnob. And we'll call you *knob*.'

That's the key line. The uppercut. There's damage, and I can feel it. They laugh hard. They laugh because they have to. I smile to mitigate the damage, which shows I'm on their side. I'm not against laughter. I try to regain control. 'As long as we can communicate, and write as we please, what's wrong with naming a town after a biscuit company?'

'It's about a corruption of language. We've turned our language into a commodity.'

'How do you expect councils to pay their bills?'

'Just like the rest of us.'

'We're not selling poison. Take a walk round Jacob's Creek. Visit Hyundai. Look at the difference we've made.'

'Do the people of Hyundai want to grow up in a car?'

'It's better than living in a ghost town.'

'It's a false choice.'

'No, it's not. You're punishing them. You

want to pull the rug from under their feet.'

'You want to name the rug *Sports Direct*.' She seems happy with this line. She's winning most of the laughs. She speaks in riffs — little one-liners that stay in your mind. More than anything, it's become a comedy contest. Kendal is smiling. She has earned the right to smile. 'You think there's nothing sacred,' she says. 'You think everything can be bottled and boxed and turned into a product. You have no respect for the human experience. You turn everything cold. All you do is convert people's hopes and dreams into profit. You know the price of everything and the value of nothing!'

The applause is such that I can only raise my voice. 'That's not true.' They're addicted to applause. They would clap almost anything so long as it had a rising, rhetorical flourish. They're young, clapping seals. If anything, the goodwill surrounding Kendal intensifies. She does nothing to squander it. She could say nothing and it would still be enough. They've made up their minds. They choose virtue over vice. Someone else can make the hard decisions. What's important is that they feel good about themselves. It feels like the end. There should be a klaxon. Some of the students stand and applaud. If they were watching a boxing match, they'd call for the bell. It's difficult to change the mood. Kendal looks at me and shrugs as if to say *shall we wrap it up?* There must be an end to everything. She offers a hand; we shake. She addresses the room and asks what they thought.

'Raise your hand if you agree with me.' There's a near unanimous show of hands — they were racing to see who could raise their hand first. 'And who agreed with Miles?'

I look at the audience. How many hands do I have? One . . . two . . . three . . . I don't have many hands.

8

STICKY TOFFEE PUDDING

I open the gate and notice the problem tree, with its growing colony of fungi. I think about whether I should make a joke about being a 'fun guy'. I decide not to. The wheelbarrow's gone, replaced with an empty shopping trolley. Trust Kendal to go on a last-minute trolley-dash for fig rolls and crackers. She said to bring nothing — the first round of mind games. She told me not to cook, and certainly not to bring flowers. If I want to be helpful, I can learn a little about the other guests — the worst task of all. Most of all, my involvement extends to coming along and making all the jokes. In the absence of music, or a sign at the door, I worry for a moment that I've got the wrong day. There's a light from the corridor. I raise a hand and knock three times. Kendal's coming down the stairs and checks herself in the mirror. I know it's going to be a long night the moment Kendal opens the front door. She's wearing a party hat and says my name in an over-animated, insincere way. It means that everyone is here and they're listening. I enter the hallway and it's only when the guests come into view that I pull the pink roses from my bag. Kendal's forced to smile in recognition that I've done a generous thing. It's a shame for Kendal; she's lost the first round of mind games. I smile and she knows why. I seem to get everyone's attention. Having met Kendal's teacher friends before, I don't believe they're terribly burdened by interaction with the male species (and probably all the better for it). One of the women rises from the bean cushion and leans to kiss me on the cheek; she manages not to spill the wine glass in her hand.

'How do you pronounce tortoise?' she says.

'Pardon?'

'Wait, wait, wait. I can't give you a clue. How do you pronounce . . . you know, that shelled creature — like a terrapin.' She makes a hand gesture to indicate *going-for-a-swim*. She still hasn't said hello.

'Tortoise.'

'Yes!' someone says.

'No one can pronounce it.'

They do a 'sorry, sorry' routine and proceed to introduce themselves again. They're teachers, but they're allowed to have fun tonight — they want to stress this point.

102

Almost straight away I've forgotten their names. Kendal passes me a glass of sparkling wine. There's a double-knock at the door and a man enters. He has a dark, receding hairline and his arrival prompts a similar sort of cheer to my own, only higher-pitched and perhaps more dishonest. Kendal points me in the direction of the new arrival, which leads to a handshake and a 'hello, mate' kind of thing.

'Miles runs a company called Lingua Franca, a naming rights agency.'

'Oh right.'

I'm immediately invited to justify myself. I proceed to explain the purpose behind Lingua Franca, and our intention to rename every town in Britain after a corporate sponsor. I mention that we're visiting Barrow-in-Furness tomorrow to mark its renaming as Birdseye-in-Furness.

'I'm going to visit you,' Kendal says, which has never been mentioned before. 'I want to see how it works.' The mind games continue.

From the other side of the room there's a sudden clamour of 'Yeah, how does it work?' I'm required to explain the process — the ribbon-cutting, changing of signs, map reconfiguration — and while they listen to what I'm saying they don't do a very good job of taking it all in. Their response is to say 'right' in order to show they're listening without endorsing anything I say. They wait for pieces of information they find problematic before deciding when exactly it's appropriate to wince.

The new arrival's brain catches up with the rest of the room — which isn't far to travel. 'Oh, I have heard about this.' He will have read about us in the free newspapers on trains. Some of the broadsheets have also featured us — often in negative column pieces — but the main reason for the media interest is the fact we're a gimmick. You often find features imagining what kind of outlandish brands could replace the names of classic British towns. When we first started, the public regarded us with a certain curiosity. We were presenting a new idea — or at least an extension of an old idea — and people seem to like newness, no matter what it entails.

'Miles is angry with me because I undermined him in front of my class.' Kendal exits the living room; she just wanted to plant a seed.

'How did she undermine you?' one of the women says.

'Just the usual stuff. My company, my commitment to evil . . .'

They laugh, because they're supposed to. I need a distraction. Something smells like chicken stock. I mention what a great job

Kendal's done with the hosting. Kendal shouts for someone to switch on the music. She calls for something else but no one knows what she's saying — it becomes a temporary source of amusement in the absence of anything else to laugh about. There's another knock on the door, another male. The triple date is underway. It starts again, the excitement and the handshakes. I end up repeating my story about how Lingua Franca came to dominate our lives. Kendal enters with a hot tray containing the stuffed chicken and roast onions. She's wearing oven gloves but she handles the tray like she'll be scalded any minute. Everyone makes a big thing of applauding the chicken's arrival. We assemble around the table, ready to accept that we might not get along very well. Things settle down; the food occupies their attention. They're not focusing on the whys and wherefores of naming rights anymore; they're focusing on roast potatoes. Kendal makes an effort to integrate the chap with the receding hairline. 'Remind me what it is you do,' she says. He takes the opportunity to mention that he works for a consumer rights watchdog. He tells everyone which electricity plan to purchase and the merits of each package. It sounds like valuable work, but not something to talk about for five minutes.

Kendal feigns interest by mentioning some-thing about the cost of heating a home — a delaying tactic, which inches us closer to the Promised Land (the night coming to an end). Midway through the first course, the rest of the table acquire a confidence they didn't possess before. It's the alcohol that's responsible. The volume increases — it's like someone has pointed a remote control at the room and turned everything up. It builds into cross-table chat with everyone's input but little in the way of engagement.

'I'm definitely having babies.' Kendal pours champagne into a flute. 'The more I think about it the more I like the name Henry. It has a patrician quality.'

Someone nudges me on the shoulder. 'There you go, Miles.' I stick my fork into a Brussels sprout. It gives me strength.

'Miles would make a great father,' Kendal says.

'No. That's not true.'

'Sometimes you forget how kind you are.' I want to look at my hands. I want to see whether there's any truth in what she said. For some reason, I think I can find the answer by looking at my hands. 'We could have a daughter,' Kendal says. 'You could pay for everything. The jewellery . . . the shoes . . . '

'She sounds lovely.'

'The only trouble is that we'd have to have sex.'

It moves onto a conversation about mortgages, the cost of living and something else. Everyone wants to say something. They suddenly have opinions about all sorts of subjects. They're talking almost as loud as they can and the effect is to neutralise anyone who wants to talk at a normal volume. It gets so loud that I'm the only one who can hear Kendal say there's more gravy if anyone wants it. It gets to the point where most of them seem to forget what they're talking about — they just want to shout. It seems to be a political debate, but I'm unable to focus on what anyone's saying. A lot of the sentences begin with 'yeah, but how come . . . ' How come they won't speak English? How come they're allowed to wear a burqa? They seem to know the answer to their own questions, as though every solution were obvious; they believe in absolutes, not nuance. Kendal seems on a state of alert. She tries to change the subject to the dessert that's on its way. Then it transpires that one of the teachers has taken great offence to something. 'What do you mean?' she says to the man opposite.

'Well, you know . . . it was a joke.'

'Do you think it's funny?'

I rise from my seat and start to gather the plates. Kendal looks alarmed. 'I'll do it, Miles.'

'It's alright.'

'No really, I'll do it.' She tries to wrench the plate from my hands. I manage to resist. I carry the plates to the kitchen. Another victory. I scrape the bones into the bin. I pull the dishwasher door open. I run the tap and start to rinse the dirty plates. I listen to their argument, which is starting to brew. It's the perfect place to listen. I'm uninvolved, like a cat sitting from a height.

The accuser raises her voice. 'Don't try and wriggle out of it.'

'Come on. Lighten up.'

No one's in the mood to *lighten up*. It sounds like he's being racist again. The two couples align on opposite sides of the debate. The triple date has become a war.

'When you use that word, do you think about what you're saying?'

'Oh come on. It's just a word.'

'It's not just a word though, is it?'

The accused is stern and unrepentant. 'It was a joke.'

I run the hot tap against a knife. I'm distracted by text messages on my phone; Nigel informs me that we're leaving at nine a.m and the Barrow officials are looking forward to greeting us. *Are you enjoying the turnips?* is the next message.

No turnips I reply.

Everyone's quiet by the time I've stacked the dishwasher and re-entered the living room. You can tell that no one's enjoying the experience of sitting at the table. The only good thing you can say is that all the noise has stopped. My strategy is clear — don't say anything, and let the others say what needs to be said. I'm on a losing game tonight, but this one's a winner. I can't lose from here. I'm taking the ball to the corner flag. I'm running down the clock. I might be able to get out of here. There's an actual chance I could leave the house as the second or third least popular person. I've gained a couple of percentage points. The accused explains that he didn't mean to cause offence, it was more the fact he wasn't thinking. 'I didn't mean all Muslims,' he says. It's agreed that the subject should be dropped. I can feel myself getting ready to sleep, which is contrary to the requirements of the moment.

The next part of the evening is dominated by forced laughter, owing to a game involving strips of paper and a hat. Kendal is laughing but she's not enjoying herself — I know this because I know Kendal. She's laughing, but she's acting. It reminds me that we're not so different. I notice that one of the guests looks at his watch. The racist says he better ring a taxi. I wonder whether to make a joke about getting a *black* cab, but think better of it. We spend the final part of the night listening to the consumer lobbyist talk about mortgages. I wonder for a moment if the subject lends itself to racism. This is also what Kendal's thinking. She looks at her watch. She says it was lovely that everyone made the effort, and we should do it again sometime. She looks like she wants to dip her face into what remains of the mashed potato.

★ ★ ★

'Everyone in Barrow knows we're on the nine forty-one,' Nigel says. 'They want to ambush us. The safest bet is to put you in Darren's van.'

'Fine.'

'That way you can avoid the egg throwers.' There are piles of notes on the desk. Nigel has been drafting the speech for the naming ceremony. 'The company line is that we're here to listen. Yes, we understand the negative publicity surrounding Lingua Franca of late, but that's a thing of the past. We want to revitalise Barrow. We want to make it special. We don't want Miles Platting to be remembered as the worst man in England.'

'You've beaten me to it.'

At this stage of a project, the side office becomes the nerve centre. The boxes have been labelled as though we're moving house. Nigel's written words like *kitchen, tech* and *fun* with a black marker pen. On the table, there's a diagram, which displays each component of the operation: press, web, admin, security, catering and travel. There's a map of Barrow-in-Furness. Barrow is roughly where I thought it would be — somewhere in the far north-west. I wouldn't want the people of Barrow to know that I need to look at the map. If you're going to obliterate a town, you ought to know where it is.

'I didn't realise how close it is to the Lake District.'

Nigel isn't listening. He doesn't really care about Barrow itself, compared with the process of getting it sold. Nigel is what they call a company man. He will be here long after the radiators.

Through the glass partition, the office maintains its slow, post-Eden rhythm. Everyone's happy to work, but not quite as motivated, perhaps. Some of them are putting on their coats in anticipation of the departure. The sales team remains focused; they're the reservists, who will undoubtedly fuck around as soon as we've gone. Outside, a team of workers instal a mesh of netting running the length of the window. It gives the impression that if anyone wants to kill themselves, they ought to think again. Nigel pulls out a sheet of paper.

'That's the speech. Learn it.' He rummages through the contents of his drawer; he asks whether I've seen the train ticket receipts. Then he mutters something about linen. These are the moments where Nigel needs to be alone. I step away so he can get on with the business of losing his mind. I'll meet him in Birdseye-in-Furness.

I instruct Darren to meet me in the underground car park. We load the van with stationery, pillows and various bits of equipment that Nigel couldn't take on the train. Darren neatly packs the medical kit alongside the tins and non-perishables. He closes the van. We walk a couple of hundred yards so I can get cigarettes. I feel very much like a politician on a walkabout with his secret-service guard.

Someone steps out from a vehicle and aims a camera in my direction. 'Do you feel bad at all, Miles?' He circles us, taking pictures. We walk exactly as we are. 'What does it say about your company that one of your staff decides to kill himself?'

'We've got nets.'

We enter the newsagent. Darren stands in the door and blocks the photographer's path. 'It's a free country,' the photographer says.

'And what?' Darren says. 'And what?'

I ask for a pack of Marlboro Lights from behind the counter. The shopkeeper looks at the commotion and tries to read my face, as if I'm the decoy. I'm not suggestive of anything. This relaxes the shopkeeper. I take the cigarettes and my change. I tend to smoke when I'm bored and away from home. Darren clears a path so I can exit. He looks at his enemy, who edges backwards, caught between his need to take a picture and his need to survive. There's another flash, which Darren objects to. They grapple for a moment. Darren grabs the photographer's collar and lifts him up. For the first time there's fear in the man's eyes. Darren carries the man a few steps and deposits him into a metal cylinder bin. Darren gives the bin a little push. He looks at me to see if he's done a good thing. I nod. We walk back through the security gate, showing our passes to the guard. I thank Darren for his afternoon's efforts.

'You alright, sir?' He calls me 'sir' when he wants to emphasise his loyalty. 'He shouldn't chat such bollocks, should he?'

'No.'

I put on my seat belt. I get myself comfortable and I tell Darren that we better drive. So we do. We head north, past towns we've privatised and those that remain intact. We pass AXA and Red Bull, Deutsche Bank and Liverpool (nothing can be done about Liverpool). The motorways of Britain are basically our canvas. You can turn off the radio or change the TV channel, but you can't ignore road signs as long as you need to know where you're going. You need to know that it's five miles to Talk Talk, and twenty-three to Sunny Delight. There's a traffic incident just outside Monster. At the Procter & Gamble service station, I feel confident enough to walk to the toilets on my own. If someone were to kill me, you'd have to give them credit. On the road we make good time. By the time we pass Waterstones, we seem to have cleared the worst of the traffic. I close my eyes in the knowledge that Darren will get me to Barrow. I think about Ptolemy and whether Kendal will remember to feed her. I think about Kendal.

We go forward, our brave battalion, in our Toyota Priuses and first-class trains. We're Lingua Franca and we're on our way. They came; they ate quinoa; they conquered. The only thing we fear is not having Wi-Fi.

★　★　★

I seem to have amassed a great number of treats while I've been writing. On my bedside table is a bar of chocolate with a sticker that says *Miles*. To my left, a mini-fridge has appeared with bottles of ice-cold mineral water. The nurse looks at me, alerted to the fact I'm no longer writing. She quickly gets out a pen.

You're doing great!

She gathers the sheets of paper and puts them in a file. For someone who claims to love my story, she doesn't seem that interested in reading it.

I pull myself into a sitting position. 'Can I go now?'

She frowns and crosses her arms, an actress doing a bad impression of an angry person.

'Seriously, can I go?'

She shakes her head like I've let down my family, my country, my planet . . . She snatches the chocolate bar and gives it to another patient. As she exits the room, I think carefully about what I've done. The only trouble is that I'm not really sure.

115

9

ALL ROADS LEAD TO BIRDSEYE

Barrow-in-Furness Town Hall has a large clock tower and a gothic sandstone façade. People descend here to celebrate important events, which doesn't happen as often as it should. The backdrop is lit with the Birdseye logo, next to Barrow's traditional coat of arms. The text says:

Introducing Barrow's new naming rights partner.

It's disingenuous, of course, to present the arrangement as a partnership. The idea is that Birdseye will replace Barrow as soon as possible. What's important is to pretend we're active participants in the town. We're indivisible from the gothic stonework and clock tower. We *are* Barrow. From one town to the next, the essence of what we say doesn't change very much. We might tailor the emphasis to one thing or another, depending on the delicacy of the moment, but the format remains constant. We're

116

treated like a rock band by the council; and we're hated by the public. You can be sure that many in the crowd aren't thinking about the event itself. The appeal is more the fact it's a fun day out; people are able to get together, which is better than getting drunk at home. On the side of the stage are trumpeters and drummers from the local army. Their presence is important, as the public don't like to boo when soldiers are around. If the military endorse what we're doing — or at least perform their civic duty in having nothing to say about anything — we can't be defeated. The brand ambassadors — a local athlete and a reformed young offender — are accompanied by officials from the Post Office, whose duty will be to erase the name Barrow-in-Furness from its Postcode Address File. The drummers and trumpeters entertain the crowd with a version of a Cumbrian song which no one seems to know. There are doves waiting to be released. It hasn't rained yet, somehow. It seems inconceivable that our launch could take place without the rain.

What happens next is the formal naming ceremony, in which the dignitaries take turns to lose everyone's attention. The mayor, in his priest-style garb and gold chains, sounds less like a leader and more like a risk analysis consultant. He talks about the opportunities for local businesses arising from new enterprise zones; he says that Barrow folk are enterprising, as if these are the qualities that are preferable to all others. The members of a local business forum — who championed the name change — applaud without interruption. The Lord Lieutenant of Cumbria leans over to write his name on the page. The signing is overseen by an elderly dame from something called the Royal Victorian Order. The mayor declares that all local businesses and public organisations are duty-bound to use the name Birdseye-in-Furness for the town hitherto known as Barrow-in-Furness. Some people applaud and others start to boo. Some proceed to shout in the direction of the stage. A school choir begins to sing in unison, and just like the military song, it has the effect of eliciting silent respect from the crowd. I almost forget my cue until Nigel raises a hand from the corner of the stage.

The mayor says, 'It gives me great pleasure to introduce Miles Platting, founder and creative centre of Lingua Franca.'

I wave to the crowd, focusing on an imaginary space where my family ought to be standing. In these situations, I have to remember that I'm not a child who's won a prize; I'm an unpopular man whose contribution to humanity has been to diminish its worth. It's difficult to gauge the nature of the crowd. It's not exactly a mob. There are too many neutrals for that. But certainly there is a minority who would probably wish death upon me. At the front is a group of middle-aged men, most of whom are determined to keep booing. My instinct is to pretend they don't understand us. Sadly, they understand us very well.

One of them shouts, 'Fucking scum!'

I place my speech on the wooden lectern. It's too late to change the words. If I had the energy, I'd modify the content. I wouldn't put so much emphasis on the moral principle. I'd let them decide whether naming rights constitutes good or evil. I'd talk more candidly about what's about to happen. There are some in the audience — the hairdressers and kebab shop owners — who will doubtless give the speech a fair hearing. They understand there's a carrot dangling in front of them. If they can see beyond brand-Birdseye, and the shame of renaming the town in honour of a frozen fish retailer, they'll understand the money-making potential of the project. A cash-rich council means more investment, more customers and more money. I could probably just purse my fingers and say 'money, money, money' and they'd know what I'm saying.

As soon as I open my mouth I feel like an out-of-town elitist. 'Barrow is moving into a new era, ladies and gentlemen. In ten years' time, you will think of Barrow as today we think of Barbados or Dubai — a major destination with a world-class international profile. That means your home values will increase, your wages will rise and new opportunities for commerce will emerge.' Enough people are applauding. It gives me the right to continue. 'I know the name 'Birdseye' might take some getting used to, but naming rights are nothing new. We're not doing anything the Romans weren't doing when they called it Londinium.' The crowd are thinking about this. There is something encouraging about the silence. They're listening, at least. They can't quite believe what they're being told, but they're listening. 'Language must change, and it changes according to our needs. We own language. Language doesn't own us.' A woman has been shaking her head almost the whole time. She hates Lingua Franca; she hates the destruction of language and community. She doesn't care if money comes into the town. None of it will do any good. She is holding a sign that says:

Barrow-in-Furness — R.I.P.

I'm of the opinion that we should provide some sort of training in emotional resilience. It's hard to observe local people's anger without feeling like you want to be on their side. It's the humanising effect. It's like showing a meat-eater around an abattoir. It's important to keep a distance. Once you're committed as deep as we are, there's no way out. 'Ladies and gentlemen, a rose by any other name would smell as sweet!' The more I speak the more I realise I've said these things before. I'm reciting a script, or someone else's poetry. It's only when I pay close attention to the human faces that I realise I don't really know what I'm saying. The words from my mouth don't match what's happening in my head. I say something about Shakespeare and I feel like I'm falling. I get a glance from Nigel, who knows better than to get involved. He waits at the side and makes no contribution other than to watch closely. He's like one of the continuity folk on film sets; his next contribution will be to mention how much I neglected to say. There's a commotion coming from the back of the crowd. Something is happening, but it will be dealt with. The challenge is to keep everyone contained to the point where they're unable to create a farce. The guards are deployed in a semi-circle from the stage outward; I'm in the middle of the horizontal line. It's a similar method to that which saved Ronald Reagan. If the enemy were to break the first line, someone would eventually take them down. Our critics like to mention that Lingua Franca benefits from subsidised policing costs. Nationalise the losses, privatise the profits. This might be true, but none of them have ever had a knife thrown at their head, which happened to me in Mitsubishi. There's a chant coming from a section of the crowd. It's indecipherable, but the tone carries a definite menace.

Lingua Franca, language killer.
Lingua Franca, language killer.

I can see their homemade placards bobbing above people's heads. There are lots of little shark fins coming towards me. They know what they want. They want tradition, community and the satisfaction of knowing they don't have to consider themselves sell-outs. They want their community to be sacrosanct, an impenetrable fortress. Each of them is free to walk ahead, parting the crowd as they go. The chanting has built into something stronger. There are more numbers behind it now. They're making all the noise. I feel a sudden jolt against my chest.

Something lands next to me. On the stage is a turnip. Another vegetable — a radish — flies over my head. These are hard vegetables, not the kind that break upon impact. A potato strikes one of the cameras. A cabbage hits the boom pole and microphone. Somehow, the stanchion supporting the camera gives way. Someone scuttles onto the stage with a dustpan and brush. The protestors are carrying bags of vegetables, which provide a good supply of ammunition. Nigel raises a hand and the trumpeters strike up a song. The army will save us. The guards begin to coordinate their movements, shrinking the space in which the protestors can move. Suddenly we have an incident. I get a glance from Nigel that says it's time to go. I need to say something that makes it look like I'm not just finishing early. I'm not meant to be scared. 'So remember! A rose by any other name would smell as sweet. Barrow is the rose, ladies and gentleman, and nothing smells sweeter than your new naming rights partner: Birdseye!'

A cauliflower almost hits my head. One of the guards attempts to block the hail of carrots. Suddenly I'm obliged to exit. We don't have to say anything else. We've said our piece for the benefit of the cameras. Someone puts a coat around my head. It's supposed to be for my own protection but it looks undignified. I'm unidentifiable, except for the fact I have a coat around my head. I must look like a criminal leaving court after a guilty verdict. I'm taken to a secure area backstage. The councillor apologises for the behaviour of his people; they ought never to express an opinion. Nigel's on his mobile phone, discussing what it all means. I'm in between two guards, whose professional duty is to get punched on my behalf. I think about what Kendal would say; she would laugh that I was pelted with vegetables. She'd say it's my own fault for inventing Lingua Franca in the first place, and it's only a matter of time until I realise what I've done. She'd say there's still time to repent. It's up to you, Miles Platting. The world is yours.

10

THE SUFFIX QUANDARY

The Walney Channel separates the mainland from our unit base. As per our requirements, the facility comprises of a temporary building for media equipment, portable toilets, recreation rooms, a static caravan canteen, medical centre, and most impressive of all, twelve shipping containers retrofitted with single beds, security slide doors and enough space for an average-sized adult. For the most part we're standing on shingles, but there's an extensive decked area on which most of the buildings have been erected. The units are made from recycled materials, with a groove in the roof designed to collect rainwater. The containers are stacked in two rows, connected by a metal staircase and walkway. The units were fitted off-site and brought here via cranes. It's a credit to the builders that they can instal the unit base in such a short time. Each of the containers is a different colour; we have our own aesthetic, which is beloved by the *Financial Times* Life & Arts section. The public erroneously believes that we carry out the construction ourselves. We're synonymous with bright colours and dynamic design. The spectacle is what matters — it would be worth choosing Lingua Franca for the spectacle alone.

The advantage of our location is that no one can get to us. From our position on the banks of the slipway, the only feasible line of attack would come from the west — from Walney Island itself. There are road blocks in place to deter any rebels and a pop-up police station at the entrance of our settlement. We're aided somewhat by the area's topography; from the water there's a steep muddy verge that acts as a buffer to anyone coming from the street. The patrol boats screen the water for any attempts at landfall. The connecting Jubilee Bridge allows us to monitor traffic that enters from Birdseye. Nigel likes to joke that we're missing a trick with all this security: the Walney Islanders might delight in their sister settlement's rebranding; they probably want to bring us cups of tea and blankets.

From the stairwell, the view is of the grim, magnificent Devonshire Dock Hall — the largest shipping hall in Britain. It's a vast, unwelcoming structure in which attack submarines are given a facial. It's one of the largest oblong buildings you could ever see.

Its purpose — in part — is to restrict satellites from being able to capture the secrets of shipbuilding assembly. You can almost forgive the scale of such a building if it were born of love — a cathedral, say — but when the purpose is to construct death ships you wonder how it ever came to pass. It's almost as if the weapons are being made in this forgotten corner of England so that the rest of the country doesn't notice. One of our mischievous arguments is that we're liberating Barrow from its reliance on the death industry. The money will attract benign businesses that do kinder things. You don't need to build weapons anymore; you can sell hot sausage rolls and cheap nylon clothes. Down below is our improvised town square. Everyone likes to congregate, play table tennis and drink beer. There's a canopy under which the staff play ironic games of chess. The dress code is relaxed, owing to the mud and rain. I can see the checkpoint allow a couple of cars through. The journalists are on their way.

The meeting room has enough space for everyone including the web developers, make-up artists, press assistants and goody-bag handlers. The photographer's job is to capture images of Nigel looking serious. There's room for the journalists, on the proviso they don't ask any questions. The table at the side features a row of upturned coffee mugs. It's the most popular thing of all, the table, and everyone seems to be looking at it. Nigel gets jealous of the table. He stands at the front with a cup of coffee. If you didn't know better, you'd think he was a chilled-out professor. I know better.

'Welcome to the unit base, from which we'll conduct the week's operations. I'd like to thank our construction partners — Keane & Sons Builders — for delivering such a magnificent site in the days prior to our arrival. As you will know, the set build ensures we can manipulate the conditions to our advantage. We can ensure your safety while maintaining an aesthetic and standard for which Lingua Franca is world renowned.'

Behind Nigel is a projected screen with a reminder of our campaign slogan:

Birdseye: Believe in a Brighter Barrow

Nigel talks about Lingua Franca, its exponential growth and its plans to grow more. He remarks on how every time we have one of these sessions, the room feels more crowded. We do a good line in talking about how great we are. Nigel proceeds to outline the events schedule; we've got radio interviews, signage consultancy and a series of meetings with local businesses. He says that if anyone needs reminding, we ought to behave in a way that befits our organisation.

'No, don't do that,' someone jokes, and everyone laughs. Nigel discusses the empirical benefits of naming rights on a local economy. He makes a couple of jokes, which get an insincere laugh. I sometimes wonder if they're laughing out of fear, like hopeless victims of a dictatorship being forced to smile with a gun to their back. Then Nigel pulls a face, which tells them something's not funny anymore.

'And as we gather today, I'd like to observe a minute's silence for Eden, who will always remain in our thoughts.' The silence is observed in different ways. The journalists stare into a respectful distance. Some of the photographers take pictures. The rest of us don't want to think too much in case we cry. Then we're released. We're allowed to walk freely and make coffee. I make it my business to avoid conversation and to listen. The dominant accent is a kind of south-east whine that belongs to nowhere. It's an accent you might hear as far west as Swindon and as north as Dermalogica. Everyone says I did a good job on the town hall speech. I might have got pelted with vegetables but I did a good job. I've set the tone. I've made it possible for the circus to execute its programme of events. I'm the ringmaster. A tired ringmaster. The journalists look in my direction, making sure I can see their accreditation badges. I've got a conversation scheduled with *The Travelodge Gazette*. I'm ushered to the corner by the make-up artist. She has a brush belt which holds each of her little make-up wands. She asks if I can face the light. My face is subject to scrutiny. I'm advised to look up so she can get a better view.

'Don't look so scared,' she says. She smiles and sticks her tongue out — briefly — in a way that's meant to be playful. Not like a lizard. She makes an effort to drag her kit box closer. She works on the outer reaches of my hairline, dusting it. She's forced to lean so high that her stomach is exposed. The belly looks at me. My eyes are closed, but I can sense I'm being watched. One of the journalists says, 'Mr Platting,' and announces that we're going to speak in a minute. I know exactly how it will go. They'll ask how it feels to be hated. They'll ask which towns are next, and whether anywhere is off limits. They'll ask what I think about emojis. They'll ask about Kendal. They'll probably know what the headline will be. *Miles Platting: I'm not evil, I'm edgy.* Then we'll take a walk by the shore and they'll try to get me to reveal a deeper side. They'll ask me to paddle in the water and pose on a rock. They'll tell me where to look and how to smile. Then I'll cock my head and turn sideways. *Nice, very nice!* I'll invite them to my little container unit and serve them beer from a fridge. *You're not so bad, Miles. Who cares what they say . . .*

★ ★ ★

We gather at the barrier that separates our bubble from what Nigel calls the animal kingdom.

'We're going on safari,' he says, unapologetic in comparing small town Englanders to baboons and chimps. We follow our tour guide, a fully vetted local. He points to the dock, where ships were first built in the 1800s. Some of the operations team aren't keeping up the pace; some are distracted, texting on their phones, or having their own private conversations. In the absence of anyone paying attention, Nigel feigns interest and asks the local to tell us more about girders, bolts and iron ore. The members of our party only start to show interest when we pass through the town centre; the web copywriter laughs at the missing apostrophe on Jaynes Fish Bar; the social media manager laughs at the orange-skinned women in the hair salon; the junior creative points at traffic and says, 'Where's everyone going? Where do they work?' They point at boarded-up pubs and downmarket retail chains no one knew existed. They compare the town unfavourably to London and its socially acceptable alternatives: Brighton and Bristol. It makes me want to rename Brighton *Tropicana*. They look at the man selling pies and they laugh out loud. They almost want the tour guide to hear. They want him to know they come from somewhere better.

'What do they do on weekends?' says the tone-of-voice guardian. He is unaware of his own intolerance when he says, 'I didn't realise Barrow was so *pikey*.'

'Birdseye.'

The tour guide keeps walking. He points out where we can get our clothes washed and dried. Then he says goodbye and it takes a few seconds for anyone to notice.

We look in the junk shop, which everyone finds hilarious. They marvel at the old trinkets, the granny crockery, defunct board games and things no one makes anymore. The salesman answers their questions, taking their enthusiasm at face value, rather than for its mocking intent. I ask the salesman what he thinks of the new name.

'Yeah, well. If it brings people to Barrow . . . '

'Birdseye.'

'Aye, Birdseye. Then . . . whatever, like.'

Nigel enters the main room, with its broken furniture, a table with hundreds of porcelain rabbits and a broken grandfather clock. It looks like the inside of someone's mind.

I wait at the exit while Nigel buys a slightly chipped garden gnome.

In the pedestrianised town centre we're joined by some journalists, who follow us into the train station. Here we are, the hottest ticket in town: Lingua Franca on tour. From a distance, what we're doing must look weird. There's something strange about the sight of a dozen men debating the position of a train platform sign. Nigel's wearing a builder's hat in case he gets struck with a hard object. The railway men who fix the lines stop to watch what we're doing. There's a photographer who tries to make some space and get a clear shot. It's fine so long as they don't have any vegetables. The sign specialist allows the drill to do its work. He pulls away and the sign holds firm.

Birdseye-in-Furness

There is a small logo accompanying the text. We applaud, which is a reminder as to the purpose of the event — to mark the renaming of the railway station. A member of the council suggests it should have a suffix that says 'formerly Barrow-in-Furness'. This is what we call *the suffix quandary*. No one wants to erase the old name completely. If you're a local person, it's difficult when you see it for the first time. It's all fine in principle, but not as an action with consequences. It's never easy to let go. A train pulls into the station and the passengers disembark. They look at the sign and some of them hold their mouth, while others shake their head. In time, they won't be so shocked when they pass the sign. It won't register as being significant. Now though, it's a big deal. It's the end of the world. It's official. Barrow is dead and Birdseye is alive. Your town has been sold. Please lend us your nose so we can rub it in something.

The events happen Birdseye-wide. Our journey is accompanied by a swarm of journalists. We visit a homeless shelter where the homeless momentarily become famous.

We visit the library, which is renamed Birdseye Library. A member of public raises the suffix quandary; we refer them to the terms and conditions.

In the local doctor's surgery, we shake hands with the community nurse, who guards the door as if we plan to force our way inside. We eventually get to meet a patient in the waiting room. She holds my arm in a grip — not because she needs to cling to something but because she wants me to listen. It turns out she lives an actual life, not a stage-managed one. Someone takes a nice picture.

We instal a plaque at the ex-servicemen's club which commemorates its renaming to Birdseye Ex-Servicemen's Club. Nigel sits next to the veterans and makes long, wayward conversation in the hope that someone might take a photo. He talks about the building because it means he doesn't have to talk about war. Nice building, he says. Really nice building. The veterans talk to us about the local youths who keep spraying the walls with graffiti. Their solution is unanimous: more discipline. A retired RAF pilot talks about the time he flew a plane at 300 miles per hour at the oncoming Luftwaffe. The Head of Content tells them how to obtain Google Analytics login details for a website they're never going to build. We end up staying for a couple of hours, which consists of talking about the weather and if it's ever going to change.

We enter the Pig & Thistle, a flat-roofed pub that's part of the same brick structure as the newsagent next door. The men sitting at the tables are focused on the big screen, reminiscent of the White House staff watching Bin Laden's assassination. But it's not Bin Laden — it's horse racing. Some of our team are smirking. The copywriter laughs at the word *premises* misspelt as *premisses*. The operations director points at the menu and asks if anyone wants the £3 steak-and-ale pie. The background noise is a never-ending hum. Lots of people seem to be shouting at the same time. Two women jostle at the bar. They're using words like 'love', but in a threatening way. There's a man at the counter who doesn't have any arms. The barmaid turns the pages of *The Sun* for him. I'm conscious that we're being watched, but no one else seems to notice. Nigel stands at the bar, doing a headcount for all the pints he wants to buy. The tone in Nigel's voice — high and mighty — means it's been a good day for Lingua Franca. We've achieved our goal of raising brand awareness while keeping local anger to a minimum. He looks at the landlady and orders a round. She doesn't smile very much.

'That'll be forty-five pun.'

'Can I pay with my — '

'You can dee as you like but it's forty-five pun.'

As far as I know, the landlady isn't aware we're the villains of Birdseye. This is just how she welcomes people from the netherworld. She doesn't know that we've killed the name Barrow, and replaced it with a nonsense term. If she knew, it would fuck her world. Most of the regulars probably hold the landlady in high esteem. She serves warm ale and allows them to sit in the pub all day. One of them has a walking stick propped against the radiator. Another man, who looks like he needs to wash his hands, has draped his overalls over the chair. There's a dog sitting in the middle. None of them get enough daylight.

I lean on the counter and ask where's good to eat. The landlady says, 'The Lamb's alright.' I ask if the Lamb is a pub or a dish. She looks at me while bending to throw something in the bin. She says nothing. Her time is finite. When I ask a question, I'd better make it a good one. I haven't asked a good question yet. I ask if there's a newsagent where I can buy cigarettes. The landlady says, 'You know there is.'

'I've never been to Birdseye before.'

'Barrow.'

One of the men looks at us and says, 'Are

you boys in the army?'

It's hard to explain what we do. We sometimes refer to ourselves as a professional branding agency, which, in the former Barrow-in-Furness, makes us sound like scum.

Nigel says, 'No. We're just visiting Birdseye.'

One of the older gentlemen shakes his stick in our direction. 'What ye calling it Birdseye for?'

'What else should we call it?'

'Barrow-in-Furness.'

The landlady says, 'If ye calling it Birdseye ye can get out noo.'

One of the drunks tells them to shut up because we're in the army. Each of us becomes occupied in a separate conversation. The situation develops. They seem to get a sense that we're Lingua Franca; we're the ones responsible for the revolution.

'You know what you should call it?' the slurring man at the bar says. 'Barrow-in-Furness.'

'In fairness,' I say, and he doesn't catch onto the wordplay. 'Birdseye has a certain ring to it.'

'It's nee Birdseye to us, man.' The gentleman is nearing the end of his pint. I get distracted for a bit. Behind the counter is a plaque in honour of a dog. Clearly, the landlady feels nothing towards humans but has a great affection for dogs. Dogs can't hurt you the way humans can. If I suggested this to her, she'd throw me to the hounds. 'I've lived here me 'ull life. It's Barrow to me, and always will be. Barrow-in-fucking-Furness.'

The main concern of the landlady is to divert their attention away from causing trouble. She's seen this before. However much the landlady frowns, she's not the type to turn away customers, even those looking to ruin her town. She just says, 'On you go, lads. Keep your voices down.'

We do our best to walk through the pub without making eye contact. On the wall is a framed shirt signed by the players of Barrow Football Club. There are pictures showing old people dancing and various get-togethers where the catering looks bad. In another town, the vintage metal signs and lantern lights would be considered cutesy. We walk further into the pub. The dominant noises are the chatter from the locals, the broad accents, which seem to become thicker, more impenetrable, the more they speak in our direction. We gather some of the creaking wooden chairs and settle down. I encourage Darren to sit on the small circular stool — a pouf, I think it's called, but I don't want to say the word 'pouf' aloud. In the middle we put a big pile of coats, our own little island. A group of men start to congregate around us. One of them has their mate in a headlock. Another one raises a powdered thumb to the other's nose; the nose takes a sniff.

'This song's focking great,' one of them points towards us. 'Come and focking dance.'

No one from our side seems to be smiling anymore. No one's interested in pointing out spelling mistakes, or laughing at the women's taste in clothes. We're in a staring contest with each other. Nigel mumbles something about key performance indicators. We're running out of chat.

'Come on, posh twats! Come and focking dance.'

'We're fine, thank you,' says Nigel.

'It's a focking great song.'

'It is a great song.'

Our Head of Brand tries to engage him in a conversation about Celine Dion.

'Fock off, Celine Dion. Focking southern conts.'

It seems to spread, the information. We're a bunch of southern *conts*. We have floral trousers and hair bands. They want to punch us in the face.

They beckon us towards their mosh pit. We look at each other. Doing nothing would appear to increase the chances of getting our heads kicked in.

'Fuck it,' says the junior creative.

We stumble through the machine smoke. There is positive momentum, a surge. Our world collides with theirs. The young drunken males lock arms around their shoulders and sing. The song implores them to feed the world and let them know its Christmastime. They bellow the words with a knowing irony — that none of them are going to feed the world. They look at us to judge whether we're worth a second chance. I'm asked to give my name. They ask what I'm doing in their pub because they've never seen me before. One of them says that St George's Day should be a national holiday.

'It should be a focking national holiday, every day of the week.'

They huddle together, singing with a beer bottle as a microphone. Some of them squint at the women in our group, deciding whether to grope. I find myself standing in the same spot, unable to get my legs started. I'm a tree trunk. I start to move and everyone starts to laugh.

'Focking dance, ya cont.'

The tone sharpens again. We're doing a passable impression of people having a good time, but there's an edge. One of the men sidles up to Karen on PR; he bumps her with his belly and puts an arm around her shoulder. Nigel looks at me with a *let's wrap it up* gesture.

'Come on, mate,' says Head of Brand, lifting the man's arm from Karen's shoulder. They all begin to swarm, turning their gaze to Head of Brand.

'Fock off you soft southern cont.' They jab a finger on his chest.

There's a 'whoa, whoa, whoa', an 'easy gents', and from their side, a gathering of men who seem outraged, but pleased to be outraged. This is where they're most comfortable — the moment just before a fight. Language can only get them so far. Bare knuckles can do the rest. Something smashes somewhere. There's the sound of chairs scraping backwards. I lift one of the barstools in case I need to ram at them like a pair of antlers.

Nigel shouts, 'Get out!'

Someone shoves Nigel. Darren puts his arm around the principal aggressor, like a football manager disputing a decision with a linesman. Head of Marketing attempts to ease Head of Brand from a headlock.

I do my fire marshal thing, shepherding the marketing coordinators and CRM specialists to safety. We retreat to the island, taking whichever bags we can. I manage to clear a path for the rest of us to run. Over my shoulder I can hear them chant, 'Wankers! Wankers!' This is what happens when worlds collide. We should have a flag, really. A flag with Lingua Franca on the front, with a latte as our emblem. We're Lingua Franca. We belong in the city and we drink pumpkin spice latte. We make new worlds, better than your own.

We can comfort ourselves with one thing. If we ever return to the Pig & Thistle, it will probably be something else: a Costa Coffee or a Little Chef. Then our work will be done.

11

METAMORPHOSIS

The walkway connecting each shipping container offers a perfect view of the harbour. From our towering position above the slipway, it looks as though man has triumphed over nature. There aren't many trees or parks, just the industrial imprint of tankers, docks and tenement housing. But here we are, with our brightly coloured shipping containers and wire fence. I peer from the ledge, high above the scene. They're carrying things like little ants in a colony. The morning's activity involves litter-picking; they've left beer bottles and cigarette packets in the hedges. Nigel watches without getting involved. He maintains his authority by instructing people on what to do and where to stand. I'd rather stand outside my little square box and watch the ships come in.

Nigel's required to raise his voice. 'Are you coming down?' He wants to know if I'm ready. I lean on the ledge and tell him I'm not coming. I'm not feeling in the mood to rename the local nursery. He asks if I've taken a paracetamol, and we exchange some words about which painkillers are the most effective. He doesn't question my honesty, although he would if he were talking to anyone else. He'd tell them to stop being such a baby. He's unable to say this. Instead, he says I should get some sleep and feel better soon. I can hear some of the others say, 'Get well soon'. I shut the door and watch them depart through the slit. The taxi firms wait by the perimeter in the hope of giving a lift. Our security team will have vetted each firm.

It's only when I'm certain everyone's gone that I emerge into the light. What a relief to be met by silence. My every movement seems audible; I can hear the crunch of stones beneath my feet. The silence is to be recommended. I almost wonder why no one's thought of it before. The scene is plain and clear — without people standing around, there's more space in which to move, more time in which to think. There's a whole island to explore. There's time and space, which seems like an extraordinary turn of events. I could walk for ten minutes without having to worry about meeting journalists. I've got time to think about other people, like Kendal. I'm able to reflect on our town-within-a-town, and whether the people of Birdseye should reclaim their own name. The first plan is to check if anyone's in the kitchen, which is unlikely but possible. The sound that disappoints me — because it means someone's there — is the sound of the fridge door opening. Someone's pulling bottles out of the fridge. Darren looks worried that I've found him. He puts down the beer bottle.

'It's alright, mate. They've gone.'

Darren peers around the corner to see if I'm telling the truth. When he's satisfied, he takes a swig of beer. He's more relaxed when Nigel's not around. When it's just us two, he can do what he wants. We're the only two people who feel responsible to each other. I suggest we should go for a walk. Darren agrees. He says the unit base is 'dry', by which he means boring. I make Darren put on his coat and we walk uphill. The wind is more of a presence now — it whistles over our heads. The path that leads onto the road isn't signposted, and isn't so much a path as a series of rocks you can tread across. There's a section where we're not supposed to walk due to the contaminated soil and the occasional unexploded bomb. There's a moment where I'm obliged to hold onto Darren for the sake of balance. For the most part it's a manageable climb. At the edge of our encampment is a sign that says *No Access*. It's a sign we've erected. Really, it should say

Don't step any further because we've got no security beyond this point. We decide to walk ahead.

'I'm getting pissed off with Nigel,' Darren says. He gives a list of things that make him angry about Nigel. Nigel thinks he always knows best. Nigel puts too much importance on irrelevant things. And no matter how hard Darren works, he never gets any credit. 'He's a fucking dickhead, man.'

I try to convince Darren that he's not a dickhead. He's just a tired man trying to run a business.

'Nah, he's a dickhead.' He has a funny relationship with language, Darren. He uses what he's got. He does well to avoid clichés when it would be tempting to use *over the moons* and *at the end of the days*. He says what he wants. He raises a couple more objections. Something about Nigel's glasses. It becomes a long list. 'I swear, if he carries on, I'm gonna . . . '

'What?'

'I'm gonna quit.' Almost straight away, he looks worried about how I'm going to react. 'Obviously, I want you to be safe, yeah? But a man's gotta do what a man's gotta do. It's about time, man.'

I remind Darren that he always says he's going to quit.

He drags on his cigarette as if the smoke were precious. 'Yeah, you're right.'

We walk by the roadside. The further we walk the more isolated it feels. You could walk the full length of Walney Island and see about five people. It's a shame I'm wearing an expensive shirt. Fashion only matters as long as there are people to see it. Darren's dressed suitably, in his hoodie and builder's jeans; I wonder where the flecks of paint came from. Our decision to walk is about curiosity, most of all. It's about being able to walk unnoticed, without anyone asking where we're going. The road has a couple of car garages, equipment sheds and a burnt-out pub. With the sponsorship money, we would hope to see the arrival of coffee houses, retail outlets and faux American diners. There's a billboard selling Birdseye. There's a road sign that says *Birdseye — 1/2 mile*. The Birdseye signs have been positioned so high that no one could pull them down. We want maximum brand value — to display Birdseye everywhere we deem worthy of the public's attention. If we could emblazon the clouds with its name, we would. We should find a way.

'Do you ever think you'll be killed?' Darren says.

'Quite often.'

I tell Darren that you never feel so alive as

when you're staring death in the face. I wonder what he thinks about the way I talk. I wonder if he thinks I'm a role model, or something to avoid being. We stop at the embankment so Darren can pick up a rock, turn to face the water and throw it far. I gather an empty can and put it in the bin.

He picks up another rock. 'What are you gonna do, then?'

'About what?'

'You look like you need a holiday.' He aims for the water and throws it thirty-odd feet. It ricochets off another rock.

'I'll be fine.'

We're distracted by the woman standing in the concrete bus shelter.

'Ain't that your wife?'

She starts walking towards us, wheeling the suitcase behind. She's wearing full-on water-proofs, like she intends on climbing Scafell Pike. She doesn't seem to care that the wind's blowing her hair back. It seems disorientating that I should see Kendal here, on a remote peninsula, rather than Stella Artois. I don't understand how exactly this has happened. In her left hand is an empty coffee cup, a relic from the other world. 'Er . . . this is amazing!' I'm not sure what she thinks is amazing. The chimney stacks . . . the mud on the riverbank . . . the wind-lashed lamp post that looks like it's going to topple. None of it seems amazing. 'I mean, it's amazing and awful at the same time. Amazing that places like this still exist. Awful that you're here. Awfully amazing.' She looks disappointed that I haven't said anything. She's invaded our space, and made little attempt to explain the invasion. She's positioned herself into the middle of our lives — our working hours — without an advance warning. 'I feel like I'm in a Ken Loach film. Look at that!' She points at the potholed road. 'Desolation. I love it.' She seems to get more romantic the further north she goes. I would hate to take her to Iceland. She puts the folded coffee cup into her suitcase. She keeps her hands in her coat pockets; the only part of her body that's remembered it's cold. 'Do you get a signal here?'

'No.'

'Amazing.' She asks Darren if he's got a lighter. He pulls one from his pocket and lights the cigarette in her mouth. 'Come on then, lads. Where are you taking me?'

★ ★ ★

'Miles, this is hilarious. I mean, it's horrific — absolutely horrific — but hilarious as well.' I drop her suitcase in my small container pod.

She walks around in a trance. She has marks at the back of her neck from where the acupuncturist has pressed too hard. 'Oh my God, you have a Frida Kahlo painting. What is Miles Platting doing with a Frida Kahlo painting?' She marvels at the hanging pendant light with its ridiculous wattage. 'It's amazing what you can do with so much dirty money. Wow, a nail file!'

'We put everything in storage.' This is my brief attempt to justify my existence. 'So it will be used again.'

'Straw man,' she replies. She opens the drawer and fondles the Ethernet cable like it has some magical quality. She fondles everything, secretly hoping to find a loose hinge or a wonky screw. She raps a knuckle on the wall like someone's hiding behind it. 'Do you ever feel a bit cut off?' She scratches the wall with her nail, hoping for it to crumble. 'I suppose colonisers don't like mixing with the colonised.' She starts running her finger along the shelf where the books ought to be. 'Here we have Miles Platting, a man who's dedicated his life to the Money God. Join Miles on his quest to discover the true meaning behind eternal mediocrity.' She talks like a voiceover artist for a movie trailer. 'Miles was once a young, optimistic English teacher, with hopes of shaping hearts and minds, until he met his beautiful wife, Kendal, who took him down the path of sin. They'd get divorced, if only they could be bothered.' I sit on the bed and watch as she walks around the room, still intent on touching everything. 'Join us for the next episode, where he tries to redeem himself and metaphorphasise into a man from an . . . *Ungeziefer*.' She continues to walk as much as the room will allow. She makes an exaggerated sigh. 'What would Kafka make of this?' She peers into an unrinsed glass with its hard Solpadeine crust. 'Anyway, I've been thinking about how you can repent. I came to propose something, but I don't know what exactly.' She sits cross-legged on the bed. 'All I know is I've come to collect you.'

'Do I need collecting?'

'You know what you want. You want to come home.'

'Kendal . . . '

'You hate all this. The halogen lights. The tweed sofas. Come on, Miles. You're a romantic at heart.' She tries to engage me in a staring contest. 'Don't feel bad about doing a U-turn. I won't mock you.'

'You will.'

'Only a little. I mean, I'm no saint, Miles. I'm not a teacher. I *was*, five years ago, but I've lost the heart. I don't know what I'm doing anymore.' She looks at me again. 'And neither do you.'

'Speak for yourself.'

'You can't act, Miles Platting. You think you're a good actor, but you're not. You're B-movie standard.' She begins to walk again. 'I think we should do something together. Let's escape. Let's find a remote island, named after nothing.' She seems pleased at her own suggestion. 'Fuck it. Let's just go to Costa Rica!'

'We'd have to learn Spanish.'

'You could colonise it. You could rename it Newcastle and make them speak like Geordies.' She smiles as she thinks about our Costa-del-Tyne. 'We could find a plot of land and open a museum. Or a gallery, or a theatre. Something you love. Doesn't that excite you?' I say nothing. She lights a cigarette and opens the door. 'How about . . . ' She draws a rainbow with her cigarette. '*The Percy Bysshe Shelley Centre of Romantic Excellence.*' She turns to face the open door and blows out smoke. She begins to walk again. She comes up with other names: *The World of Byron. Byron Burger. The Wordsworth Institute. The Ministry of Silence.* 'We could be the mad husband and wife who run the place. We could be Adam and Eve. Antony and Cleopatra.'

'Henry VIII and Catherine of Aragon.'

'Kendal and Miles. John and Yoko! Let's climb under the covers and tell the world how to live.' She lifts the duvet cover and slides her body underneath. 'Coming up next, Miles Platting, language killer, transforms into Miles Platting, custodian of language . . . custodian of life!' She lies on the bed for a while, looking at the ceiling with her mouth wide open. 'Unleash your inner romantic, Miles. What would William Blake do?' She lies for a little longer, always smiling. 'I love this place. It's batshit.' Then she goes downstairs and pours herself a glass of water from the tap marked *ambient*.

★   ★   ★

They return in the evening; their mood is upbeat, a glorious homecoming after winning a battle. I can hear them opening cans of beer. Nigel can see me leaning on the metal banister. 'A great success!' he shouts. 'We got the library and the swimming pool. They're all at it. Not a single dissenting voice.' He can't stop smiling. 'Come and have a beer!'

'Kendal's here.'

'Oh.' His smile has been reduced somewhat. 'Bring her down.'

'Maybe in a bit.'

I step back so Nigel can't see me anymore. In the pod, Kendal turns away as she gets undressed, which shouldn't feel weird, but does. She puts on my dirty T-shirt. It feels right that she's wearing my clothes. It feels right that she smells like me. We light the small cheap candle, then use it to light the others. I look at Kendal and it makes me forget what happened between us. It's different, looking at her in this light. It reminds me of the old days. Here she is, taking my hand, and guiding me onto the bed. She's come to see me. She knows that I'm lost and knows where I need to go. She pulls the seam of my shirt, rubbing the cotton. I don't know what I want, except to see what happens. She guides my hands onto her waist, the warm rubber ring. I allow myself to be held. It would be good if life were always like this — a slow rocking hug. She unbuttons my shirt and throws it on the hard pine chair. She lifts the duvet cover and we go under. Every now and then, there's the sound of laughter from the courtyard. They're playing a game of cards or something. We tell ourselves they're not laughing at us, no matter what sounds we make.

12

DAFFODILS

Eden knew the building well. He had sufficient privileges on his key fob to access most parts of it. He was always the keenest to collect parcels. He knew all the other floors; he was on first-name terms with the women from the travel agency, and sometimes went for drinks with the recruiters. He knew a coffee machine on the eighth floor that had better beans than ours. He knew the names of the security guards, the outsourced electricians and the man who came to fix the leak. He knew how to get on the roof.

I sometimes wonder what it was like for Eden, in the seconds before the fall. It must have been harder in the seconds before than in the actual moment.

I reach out and feel someone's hand, which belongs to the nurse. She writes a note.

Are you alright?

The lights are off in the hospital ward. I'm in a dark hospital room and I can't find Kendal.

I'm covered in A4 pages with my handwriting. Kendal would laugh at all my written papers, the stream of consciousness hanging off the bedstead. I write to ask if I could speak aloud because I can't narrate everything by hand. The nurse shakes her head.

When will I be discharged?

You're not ready yet.

I look at the rest of the bay and get the sense that I'm the only one who's alive. The other patients are asleep, although you wouldn't know the difference if they were awake. The air conditioning unit interferes with the silence: it's the loudest thing in the room.

Have you seen Kendal?

The nurse shakes her head. For all I know, Kendal could be running through the hospital, searching each room for Miles Platting, presumed dead. She could be back in Stella Artois, leading the press campaign in honour of my memory. She could be angry, and never want to see me again. She might have organised a practical joke. She might jump out from behind the curtains and shout: *Gotcha!* She might have fallen in love with someone else. She might still love me, and not know how to say it. I seem to have overheated.

Can you help me find her? I want to do the Wordsworth thing . . .

Miles. Go back to sleep.

She doesn't want to listen anymore. I'm not being a very good patient. I rest my head against the pillow and realise I won't be able to sleep with all this silence. The only thing I have the energy for is to stay awake. I close my eyes and try to breathe in some kind of rhythm. It's not going very well.

'Fuck this,' I say aloud, to no one, as it turns out. I wipe the sleep from my eyes. I manage to pull myself up. I gather the sheets of paper — hundreds of words detailing my story, sometimes in note-form, and sometimes with a poetic flow that makes me proud to look at it. Well done, Miles. I put on the dressing gown and slippers. I do nothing, on the assumption that someone will accompany me to the toilet. No one comes. I look around at the patients. I don't think I'd wake anyone even if I pulled out a chainsaw. The cleaner remains on the ward. She mops the floor and appears permanently low, like some invertebrate that hasn't developed the ability to stand. The corridor lights flicker. I'm in a fucking zombie film. I don't want to be in that kind of movie. I want to be in a romantic comedy. I time my walking pace against someone else's footsteps so that I can avoid detection. In one of the rooms there seems to be a commotion; someone's shouting, and the nurses say, 'Shhh.' All the nurses seem to be gathered there. I hear the pull of a curtain and the door closes shut. I approach the emergency exit. It says the door is protected by an alarm — I push it, and it isn't. I emerge into a courtyard. Just opposite is another U-shaped block made from cheap red bricks. Only one of the rooms is lit. I wonder if Kendal's in there, and whether I should throw a pebble and get her attention, like something from my rom-com. I could open out my arms and say, 'Let's go to Costa Rica!' I walk along the paved perimeter, avoiding the wet grass. A blue sign makes reference to *Furness General Hospital*. The building didn't seem significant when I first arrived here: it seemed like an ugly brick hospital, built in the seventies, and that's how it seems now. A few yards in front of me is a man dressed in a robe, holding a candle. He's followed by a slow procession of robed men and women. I decide to step behind a bush and watch from a distance. They walk along a candlelit path, a gathering of robed men and women. Some of them shake bells. All of them say nothing. A little further ahead is the candlelit summit, a magnetic force drawing them in. The candles lead the way forward. They emerge from the gymnasium. There's a light from the entrance, where the procession seems to be coming from. I walk to the back exit, which has a lit window. I lean against the door and get the sense it would disturb whoever's on the other side were I to open it. I pull myself onto a ledge and peer through the window. There's about fifty people sitting in rows as if it were a school assembly. Some of them have blankets. A light shines from the projector fixed to the ceiling. I can't tell what they're watching, but they're looking at the screen. From the reflection, it looks like a black-and-white film. It has subtitles. The robed men and women are standing against the wall. They watch the audience like exam invigilators on the lookout for cheating. From behind the glass, it's hard to make out their faces. I look a little closer and it makes no difference. Starting from the back, each row is instructed to rise when it's their turn to exit. The robed instructor taps each end-of-row at a time. They rise and scrape their chairs inward. The pace quickens; the room begins to empty and it resembles a fire drill. Where's everyone going? They seem to be heading in the same direction. I think for a moment about what exactly I'm doing standing on a ledge and looking at a gymnasium in the dark. It's a strange way to spend an evening. From behind me someone blows a whistle and clangs a bell. I turn around and keep my balance. Just below is a white-haired gnome of a man, who wouldn't look the slightest bit intimidating were it not for his heavy, bronze bell, which could cause some damage. He blows his whistle and points to where he wants me to stand. I jump back down and my slippers squelch on the wet grass. He whistles like he's discovered me in a hiding place.

'Alright, man, alright.'

'Shhh,' he says, like I've said the worst thing in the world. His eyes tell me he's alarmed. Something's wrong and I shouldn't be here. I open my arms as though I'm remonstrating with a tennis umpire who's made the wrong call. We look at each other and we don't have anything to say. He doesn't even have any paper.

'What, then? What?'

All he can do is point to his own lips. He

pulls a shortwave radio from his pocket and taps the speaker three times. Three taps must mean something: *I've found Miles Platting.* Seventeen taps must mean something like *get me some screws for the new shelving unit.* His eyes are focused on mine; he looks at me as if I'm a dangerous man hiding a concealed weapon. Another man walks towards us: a much younger man in a fluorescent coat, who notices my gown and slippers. He looks alarmed too. He attempts to communicate with me using his hands. He crosses two of his fingers and flattens his palm. We speak a different language. I reply with a shrug. He points towards the hospital block where I came from.

'Oh, do you want me to go back there?'

He doesn't say 'shhh' — he just looks at me like it's a stupid question. He turns to the robed official as if to confirm whether I'm stupid. We walk to the hospital and enter via the main reception. They point to the doormat so I can wipe my feet from all the mud. I feel like an unwanted guest, the idiot who ruins a party. I say goodbye to the robed official, which he doesn't like. We enter the foyer and the guard looks for someone to dump me with. The guard seems to think we should wait, as it would be rude to step into the nurses' territory. He looks at the out-of-date magazines on the table in the hope I might want to read them. We stand in silence until the nurse arrives. A different nurse. Not even the grey squirrel. She wipes her forehead and feels her back as though it's strained. She looks at me, the incoming idiot, the waste of a bed, and looks at the guard for a translation. I glance at the magazines. Most of them have pictures of women on the cover: women's magazines, with women on the front, and men's magazines, with women too. The header says:

20 ways to get a flawless post-baby body

I think the hospital's commitment to silence would be better served if they laid out copies of *David Copperfield* and *The Master and Margarita*. The guard looks at the nurse and makes a quick gesture with his hands. She nods. The conclusion seems to be that the guard should accompany me to the bay. We walk, which I'm happy to do. I'm relaxed and compliant, which removes anyone's right to complain. The zombie lights in the corridor still flicker. We walk a little further and the nurse seems agitated as we pass one of the rooms. She puts an ear close to the door. From within there's a strained, distant voice. I think he's saying, 'This is an outrage!'

There's a commotion, the sound of chairs scraping. The door handle turns and another nurse steps out, looking like she's been running on a treadmill. 'I want a lawyer!' is the next line. The man shouts something about everything being a disgrace. It's nice to hear language, the real, spoken kind. It feels good to have an accomplice, a comrade, someone else who thinks the place is crazy. I want to shout back, so it can be like two birds tweeting.

'Hello, hello!' There's a pause of a couple of seconds. He shouts something back, indecipherable. I need to conjure more strength in my lungs. I might as well be underground again. 'Hello, HELLO!'

The nurse claps her hands, an improvised gesture designed to distract me. I keep my eyes on the door. There's another shout from inside but the words are indistinct. We're almost talking through a tin can telephone. The guard puts a hand on my shoulder but I manage to shake it off. I think about what Kendal would say in this situation. She would put on a voice: effete Kendal.

'You cannot silence the heart. Try as you might!' The guard grabs my shoulder, turning into a nightclub bouncer. He leads me down the corridor. 'Unhand me, good sir!' There's a smile on my face, which they don't like, even though I'm speaking in smiles. We walk down the corridor; the guard makes a point of showing me the sign that says *Silence Please.* 'Yes, I know. Silence.' I decide to say it in a French accent. '*Silence!*' It's a French word: silence. I think of other French words in English. *Fiancé, Debacle.* 'Could you tell me how you say *debacle*?' The guard sighs; it's been a long day. He grabs my arm and gives it a squeeze. Nothing too hard, but a squeeze nonetheless. They take me into the bay and I decide it's time to sing. '*It's only words, and words are all I have, to take your heart away!*'

'Shhh,' the nurse says. She points to the other patients as though it were rude of me to sing. I move with grace. I hold the curtain and clutch it close. '*Da dadadadadada. Da dadadada, da!*' The guard tugs at my arm. '*It's only words, and words are all I have, to take your heart away!*' I wave my hands in the style of a conductor leading a string section. Then I take a bow. I don't have an audience, though. I have a few words from the Bee Gees (later Boyzone). I have a guard and a nurse, whose arms are crossed, and some tired hospital patients who want to sleep through the whole thing. The nurse almost looks like she's going to cry. For all I know I might have ruined her birthday. I could take it further if I wanted. I could cause some damage. I could start pulling plugs from the machines; I could start singing ABBA. The doctor enters, the grey squirrel. I open my arms to say, 'Woe, destruction, ruin and decay! The worst is death, and death will have his day!' I do a little walking routine, as though I were leading a marching band. I keep going until I feel like I've started to depress everyone. The doctor pulls up a chair and sits beside me. She looks at me straight on. She writes a quick note which says:

I believe in you, Miles.

She puts a hand on my shoulder. I don't get a right of reply.

You'll get better soon.

She looks at me without averting her gaze. She passes me the hot-water bottle from the side. I watch the guard and the nurse, who no longer seem on edge; they're relieved they don't have to hear me sing anymore. I watch the squirrel, who watches me. I don't really want to feel like an alien. I want to live on the same planet as them.

'I'm going to bed,' I announce. 'I mean . . . ' I lean onto the bedside sheet of paper.

I'm going to bed.

I climb under the covers. I pull the duvet up to my chest and the doctor smiles. This feels good. I pull the eye mask from the bedside drawer, lift it over my head and blacken out the world. I let my legs stretch. I exhale, close my eyes, and the only thing that stops me sleeping is how bad I feel about disturbing their evening. *Da dadadadadada . . .*

★　★　★

Eden landed on a salt grit container. It was fortunate that no one was standing nearby. By the time we made it downstairs, someone was already knelt at his side. He still wore his entry pass around his neck. There was no conceivable chance he'd survive. The impact was such that no one could have lived. A cat might have. Ptolemy might have. The engineer positioned Eden flat on the pavement and shouted for help. Eden was pronounced dead at the scene. It all happened as quickly as you could hope for, in the sense there was no hope. We watched it all from the window, and we knew not to hope.

I wake up again. I'm conscious that I'm too hot. I've been sweating more than normal. I'm lying in my hospital bed, which is fine, and necessary. I feel conscious, certain of my wits. I look at my fellow patients, who seem just as comatose as before. I'd like to apologise, but they wouldn't know how to receive it. I start thinking about the nursing staff and whether I should write them a letter. I should think of them as humans, rather than robots that annoy me. I'll wake up early and write them a letter to explain my behaviour. I'll write about how I miss Kendal, and most of my mood swings can be linked to that. I'll ask if we can turn a new page; literally, in fact, so I can finish the story. I owe them that much. I'd like to talk about where we are, and whatever it is we're committed to. We could talk about the silence.

13

THE FOG ON THE TELIRE

'Are you excited?' Kendal sits on the suitcase to squash it all in. 'I haven't seen you smile like this in years . . . Are you excited?'

'I am.'

'Just say you're excited!'

'I'm excited!'

'*Más Tico que el gallo pinto.*'

I'm happy that she's still wearing my T-shirt. It reminds me of what mornings used to be like. Her hair has been flattened in places, owing to the hard mattress and the almost featherless pillow. 'Did you know more than ten per cent of the world's butterflies live in Costa Rica?' She begins to tidy the room like she's getting ready to leave right this minute. 'It's one of the happiest places in the world. And it doesn't have an army.'

'The butterflies can protect us.'

Kendal walks around the room, observing the empty bookshelf. She complains about the lack of light and opens the door ajar. I complain about the light. The pod isn't suitable for more than one person. It doesn't have the dimensions to make for a pleasant stay. She feels the inside of her coat pocket and pulls out some receipts. 'Sandals!' She writes *sandals* with a chewed-up biro. 'And sunglasses.'

'And a pet passport.'

'Where are we gonna get sunglasses in Barrow-in-Furness?'

'Birdseye.'

'Miles. Get with the programme. You've done enough damage for a lifetime. We're not having another fifty years of you fucking up the world.' She wags her biro in my direction. 'Suntan!'

'*Sí señorita.*'

She holds out her arm and points. 'Look at us. We're pale as fuck.'

'Racist.'

'I need some sunshine, Miles. Too much time on this island makes you go fucking mad.' She walks around the room and winces like she's misplaced something. She lifts the corner of the mattress. 'Earrings,' she says to herself. 'You'd think it'd be hard to lose something in this room. It's only six feet fucking long.' She reaches down at an angle — a lucky dip — and pulls out Eden's letter. 'Is this your speech?'

'Yes.' I grab it back. I want to change the

frequency. I mention that Nigel will call for us in a second.

'I think we should call it the Wordsworth Institute.' Kendal sprawls on the bed as though we're going back to sleep. 'A library of infinite wisdom curated by Miles and Kendal — plus special guests.' She lies back with her arms in the shape of an angel. 'Rooms available. No flash photography. Strong language.'

'Can I make cider?'

'Yes! Good, Miles. You're getting the picture. You can stamp on all the apples you want. And we'll be free. Free as a pair of high-flying birds!'

I recognise the knock at the door because it comes from a feeble fist. 'Alright there, chaps,' Nigel says. He doesn't make eye contact with Kendal. 'I'm not intruding, am I?' Nigel doesn't have the tact to know when he's intruding, which means he's intruding the whole time. He doesn't seem comfortable that Kendal's only wearing a T-shirt and underwear. 'They'll be arriving in five minutes.' What Nigel means is that we ought to get ready and stop wasting time. He likes to be rude in a polite way. 'Have you written a speech?'

'No. I mean . . . '

'Well, think of something nice to say. They

don't just give the Golden Submarine to anyone. It's their equivalent of the Légion d'honneur.' He makes a face which says *are you even listening, Miles?* He laughs aloud, and tries to make a joke of it. Kendal just looks at him. Nigel hangs at the door, an uptight shrew, not knowing when to leave. He notices our lack of interest and this time his face says *I'll leave you guys to it.* He closes the door as carefully as he can.

Kendal looks at me. 'He's an odd man, isn't he?'

'He just needs a girlfriend.'

She runs the tap and washes her face in the sink. She doesn't want to use the communal shower, which involves a long barefoot walk across the stones. She doesn't want to participate in any conversation while wearing a towel.

'Well, now's your chance to repent, Mr Platting. You don't want to be a wrong'un no more. Just tell them you're moving on. You need to set up the Wordsworth Institute. Costa Rica's calling.' Kendal opens the drawer and removes one of my hoodies. 'You don't have to renounce your fucking throne. Just thank everyone and admit that all good things have to end. And bad things.'

Nigel shouts, 'One minute, everyone!'

She pulls out some jeans. 'Right. I'm going

to drink some Prosecco. Then I want to see you here at two. We're off. Vamoose. Do we have a deal?'

Her forehead is wrinkled: a contingency frown in the event I say no. But I say, 'Deal.'

'Fab!' She peels off the bed sheets, suspicious of the sweat. 'You never used to sweat this much.' She smiles like she's remembered something. 'You never told me about your birthmark as well.' The way she looks at me means I'm meant to take offence. She's seen me naked, in a new context, and treats this detail like she's got something on me.

'I've always had it.'

'I'd never noticed.'

'It's always been there.'

'I suppose we used to turn the lights out.'

★ ★ ★

Our emergence into the light is a cue for everyone to look at us. Here we are, like a pair of newlyweds on a balcony. We command their attention. We're the main thing to focus on. The next sight we encounter is Nigel pulling a table; he instructs a caterer on where to put the chicken satays. The builders are reconfiguring the canteen walls so that everything's more open plan. Behind a line of tape is an improvised beach and a gazebo where the sponsors can drink. Darren's helping to clear the table so that one of the assistants can place down the salad. The set-up is typical of our wrap parties: we invite local caterers to serve olives and to make peace. We stage a meet-and-greet for town officials, sponsors, community groups and journalists. The purpose is to achieve a resolution — an official handover from which Birdseye can survive without our invigilation. It's 'mission accomplished', a pat on the back. We walk down the stairwell just as the taxis are pulling in. We're offered a flute of champagne from a waitress whose cheeks will soon hurt from all the smiling. Nigel stands at the perimeter and welcomes each guest with a handshake. By the rock pool, a man rests his guitar case on the pebbles; there's a drum kit on the edge of the breakwater. Someone serves smoked salmon on rye bread. It doesn't take long for the likes of Darren to relax and, for the sake of the occasion, pretend he's having a good time. It seems that most people are able to make conversation without the need for formal introductions. Kendal talks to some of the councillors, who seem charmed, if a little confused. She asks the local MP what he does for a living. She laughs when she finds out. She doesn't avert her gaze from the men and women with Birdseye logos on their lapels. She wants to get inside their minds. She wants to know why they woke up one morning and wanted to rename Barrow-in-Furness in honour of frozen fish. She makes conversation with our localisation team; they talk about transcreation, and whether or not you can ever faithfully translate a language. Kendal talks about Joseph Conrad: how he read in French, thought in Polish and wrote in English. They all seem to laugh and Kendal officially becomes *one of them*. Kendal asks about their roles within the company, and she doesn't seem capable of listening for more than five seconds without asking a big question; usually it's about the ethical dilemma of working for a company committed to the sale of the English language. They don't know how to respond. They weren't trained for this question in their induction packs.

'I mean, I would expect dear Miles Platting to be fully committed to evil, but you guys seem like thoughtful human creatures.'

She then focuses her attention on the canapés: she loves the whitebait and says as much. 'How much are you being paid, then?'

she asks the waiter.

Nigel finds it difficult to carry out his duties while Kendal continues to talk. He looks at me in an attempt to ascertain whether I can hear what she's saying. He doesn't like the fact that Kendal's able to speak. He thinks she should be muted. Every so often, he looks in my direction to indicate that I really ought to intervene; I shouldn't let Kendal ruin the show. I'm happy to lurk and watch from a distance. A part of me wants to shout as loud as I can about how it's all a sham. I want people to know that Lingua Franca is worse than anyone imagined, that Eden was the best worker we ever had, and that Costa Rica is where it's at.

Kendal's kept a safe distance from the gazebo by the sheer number of us. She makes a beeline for the Mayor of Birdseye, at which point Nigel steps in front of her. 'I don't think that's a good idea.'

'Oh, sorry, Nigel. You're standing in my way.'

Nigel holds up his arms like a hostage, a strange way of displaying his refusal to hit a woman, or something. She tickles his belly. He recoils and shouts, 'Miles!'

I'm involved now. I'm part of the discussion. She puts a hand to her forehead and does a damsel in distress routine. 'Oh,

Mr Platting. Come and save me from this Sheriff of Nottingham.'

'Miles . . .'

'Dearest Nigel. I know that your mad hatter's tea party means a great deal to you. But have you not considered the small matter of your legacy to humankind?' Kendal walks in a circle around Nigel. He's obliged to follow her footsteps. 'You might have made lots of money, Sheriff, but what's happened to your soul?'

Nigel stares at me for long enough so that I might reasonably ask what he's staring for.

It's my turn to say something. I aim to speak loud enough to be heard, but only by a select few. 'I think she's got a point . . . hasn't she?'

I look down at the pebbles and people's feet. I know that Nigel will be looking at me. I know what his face will be trying to display: incredulity.

Kendal steps onto the wooden deck. She talks aloud, like an actress. 'It is a rich language, Lieutenant, full of the mythologies of fantasy and hope and self-deception — a syntax opulent with tomorrows.'

Nigel points a finger at Kendal. 'Get down and stop being a nuisance!'

'Have you ever been held, Nigel? I mean, really held . . .'

'Miles!'

'Am I not being reverent enough? I do apologise.' She steps off the stage and takes a swig of champagne.

I step back so I can get the waiters' attention and distract myself in a conversation about different types of cheese. Nigel looks around as if to assess his options. In the absence of my involvement, he seems to relax. He notices that people are looking: conversations are being dropped, and they're starting to listen. He touches Kendal's shoulder like they're mates having a chat.

'Tell me what you think we should do, Kendal. I'd love to hear it.'

He seems to prefer the idea of talking to Kendal than letting her drift elsewhere. He wants to contain the virus. I'm directed by one of the PR team to a small gathering of women, all of whom wear purple T-shirts with a logo that says *Birdseye for the Blind*. One of the carers introduces me to a young blind woman. I reach out a hand so she can feel it. Miles Platting, heals the blind. They look at me like I'm a famous actor and they're meeting me backstage. Some of them seem shy; some of them giggle. They ask how the event has gone from our perspective, which reminds me I'm supposed to feign some sort of interest in this whole thing. I tell them it's gone well. They seem happy it's gone well.

'Oh, it's great to meet you,' one of them says. 'We just wanted to thank you for coming to our town. We needed a shot in the arm and you've given it.'

I keep my hands clasped on the young woman, who smiles. Behind me I can hear Kendal shout something about injustice. Nigel says she doesn't know the meaning of the word.

'Thanks to Lingua Franca, we now have the council funding to pay for assistive technology and liaison officers,' the carer says. 'You have no idea how much difference you've made.'

'Thank you. That's ever so kind.'

They talk about new opportunities and the importance of guaranteed funding. They hope to be able to provide visual awareness training and specially trained guide dogs. Over my shoulder I can hear Kendal say something about Nigel having a heart of stone.

'Miles! Come here please.'

I make a facial expression that suggests I'm reluctant to leave the conversation, but professionally obliged to. They decide to release my hand.

'Off you go, Miles. We know you're a busy man. Lovely to meet you. And congratulations. You fully deserve that Golden Submarine.'

The waiter offers them more champagne and they seem to think the whole thing is amazing. I watch them shake hands with the sponsors, who appear touched by it all. I dare say — and I never *dare say* anything — the sponsors look like they might cry. This is their gift. And it's a gift that hardly anyone could do themselves. Kendal couldn't. In a way, this is part of their package: give your name to a town and make a difference. In exchange for their name, they can help build roads, clean rivers, and comfort the blind. They can build a world where cynicism and love have found a perfect union. Oh God . . .

I turn around and find Kendal prodding Nigel's chest with her finger. 'Fuck you.' The words come from Kendal. 'Fuck Lingua Franca.' Nigel tries to laugh, but Kendal gives him no license to. She doesn't give the impression that she's making a joke. 'You might have made money but you don't have any soul.'

Nigel puts on a stern, company face, the kind he might use for a rude customer. 'Mrs Platting, here are the facts. Our towns have the best schools. The best childcare. The best end-of-life care. The best health and nutrition. The best roads and railways. The best places to eat and drink. And if you don't believe me, I suggest you ask your husband.'

They both look at me at the same time; they both want my endorsement, as if they're two bickering children in competition for a parent's approval. For once, I'm worth something. I'm one half of Lingua Franca, and one half of what was once a marriage.

I look at both of them and say, 'I'll let you two settle your differences.'

Kendal notices I don't look as excited as I probably should be. The look on my face conveys everything Kendal wouldn't want to see: indifference. She's trying to start a revolution and I've only brought a water pistol.

'Could I have your attention please?' says the Mayor of Birdseye. Everyone's instinct is to look at the mayor and hush for silence. The mayor puts on his spectacles so that he can read from a sheet of paper. 'Nothing gives me greater pleasure than to stand before you on this very special occasion. It goes without saying that Barrow, as it was, will never be forgotten. We were a proud town then, and we're even prouder now. Today, our town is synonymous with a world-class brand and we hope to uphold the standards of excellence for which Birdseye is world-renowned. In particular, there are two individuals I'd like to thank. Nigel, whose determination and rigour left us in no doubt as to the viability of this project. And Miles, whose vision and creativity is helping to transform towns up and down the country.' He asks if Nigel and I could make ourselves known and accept the Golden Submarine award for all our hard work. The applause carries us along. It's easier for Nigel, who lives for this kind of thing. I look across the crowd and catch sight of Kendal, whose arms are folded. I let Nigel go first. Nigel shakes hands with the mayor, who puts a medal around his neck. His assistant passes another medal and the mayor does the same to me. Here we are, the old team: Nigel and Miles, the Lennon and McCartney of the naming rights world. I bring the vision and he brings the business acumen. We both bring the bullshit. Nigel prods me on the back so that we're both facing the direction of the cameras.

'Thank you so much,' Nigel says. He starts with a thank-you directed to the people of Birdseye-in-Furness. We've been touched by the warmth and hospitality displayed by this great Cumbrian city, he says. We're honoured to have created a legacy upon which Birdseye can grow. The town will be more prosperous, more confident, more certain of the future. One of the great privileges of our work, the plonker goes on to say, is that we can visit different parts of the country and appreciate the rich tapestry of cultures across our sceptred isle (yes, he quotes Shakespeare). 'Together, we can look forward to a bright new dawn for Birdseye-in-Furness. Tomorrow's Birdseye will be brighter than today's. As for Lingua Franca, we're making history — big time. We've reached the tipping point, the point at which Lingua Franca becomes a national institution. It's only a matter of time before we secure a blue-chip client — an Oxford or a Bath. Go back to your office desks and prepare for Sunderland!'

They applaud, but they don't know why. We're being applauded for our existence. I'm handed the microphone. Nigel looks at me, eager to detect some kind of reasoning from my face. He wants to know what I'm thinking, and whether I'm still good to go. I scan the audience and notice Kendal standing near the sea.

'Thanks, everyone.'

Somebody whoops. 'Go Miles!'

I look out onto the rocks, the rare blue sky and the town in the distance. I try to make a joke about never winning anything in my life, but I get stuck in the words and I have to repeat myself. I have nothing to say, so I look at the Golden Submarine, which is exactly as described, but probably not gold. I'm expected to say something nice. The look on

Kendal's face says *don't you dare.* Nigel seems anxious that I might drop the microphone. In front of me are the women from *Birdseye for the Blind.* One of them is recording my speech on their phone. I could say almost anything and they'd applaud. They look like they're proud of me; they want to give me a hug. I can feel my hand getting numb, so I put it in my pocket.

'Thanks, everyone, for this award. I'm speechless. Quite literally . . . ' If Nigel were near enough, he'd step on my foot. 'I started this business with Nigel five years ago, and if someone told us we'd rename almost seventy towns in the UK, I don't think . . . well, I'm certain we wouldn't have believed it.' I try to look at no one. It feels like I'm giving a speech at my own funeral. Here lies Miles Platting, who loved life, and language, some of the time. 'I'd like to dedicate this award to Eden, our colleague who passed away just recently. We miss him very much.' Everyone applauds, even Kendal. I seem to have hit the right note. 'So thank you, everyone. God bless you. And long live . . . Birdseye-in-Furness.'

Everyone begins to clap. It's not completely unfair that I should take the applause. I wouldn't want Nigel to take the credit on his own. A plague on both our houses, or none at all. I look at Kendal, who seems to have slumped somehow — her shoulders have dropped. Her head is down. She doesn't look at me. She can smell bullshit. She knows when I don't really mean what I'm saying. If she were standing closer, she'd tell me to wind my neck in. She'd poke me in the ribs. My objective is to reach Kendal and find out the damage. What makes it harder is the bank of bodies in my way: everyone wants to shake hands. I seem to be shaking hands with someone every five seconds. People are saying 'well done' and 'congratulations'. I do my best impression of a grateful recipient. My smile manages to hold in place. The volunteers seem to come alive: this is their moment. I'm led into a press enclosure behind an advertising hoarding. We do a staged handshake and someone takes a picture. There's a queue of council officials waiting to talk. They want to take it in turns to shake my hand. I'm introduced to the local parish councillor. I begin to lose focus.

'You've started a revolution,' he tells me. 'You've shown how councils can cut their cloth and survive.' He talks about incoming investment from multinationals, property developers and companies named after acronyms. They all want to own a piece of Birdseye — an exciting Opportunity Area.

For its part, the council wants the money to build sixth-form centres and health facilities, albeit with the Birdseye logo written on the wall. 'Did you know the old Barrow was once known as the English Chicago?' he tells me. 'That's what we need to recreate.'

'Right.' I look like I'm sulking. I think he mistakes this for self-assurance. He thinks I'm used to the praise, that I can't wait to head to the next town.

One of the volunteers says, 'Please walk this way. We need to take some photos.'

We're taken on a walk along the shore — a lap of honour. The walk takes us to the site perimeter, away from our main settlement, towards a rock pool and a small cave. If it were a wedding shoot, this would be the secret garden. The photographer wants us to stand so the Devonshire Dock Hall is behind us. I try to smile as best as I can. In some of the pictures I'm probably looking the wrong way, trying to see where Kendal's gone.

'You did a good job,' Nigel says in the row behind me. 'Just keeping smiling.'

★　★　★

In the after-party, most of the noise comes from those designated to clean, and the murmur of whoever's sitting under the canopy. It's no longer a loud party vibe — it's more like a campfire chill-out, with red wine, candlelight and the lightly plucked strings of someone who's brought an acoustic guitar. Nigel claps and calls for an *expression session*. The team assemble, roughly in their departmental tribes and look nervous to be called upon at such short notice. Nigel smiles and says it's been a great week for Lingua Franca. 'I'm proud of what we've achieved, and what we've accomplished together,' he says. 'You've all embodied the Lingua Franca spirit at each stage of this journey.' I excuse myself by saying I need to check on Kendal. Nigel gives a thumbs up, which seems strangely supportive. I keep walking and all I know is that I never want to watch another *expression session*. It's the worst thing in the world, or pretty close. It's nice to walk next to the water and not have to pose for a picture. The water doesn't ripple or lap at stones — it seems content in its flat normality. From this distance, the town could be anywhere. Lamplight can make the ugliest of places look beautiful. The lights in LA aren't so different from the lights in Birdseye. I look back towards the campfire, where everyone listens to the press team describe the day's accomplishments. Next it will be the tech team's turn: they will report a spike in traffic, thousands of new backlinks and a high volume of keyword searches for 'Birdseye-in-Furness'. The accounts team will say it's business as usual, and we're on track to make December's revenue forecast. Throughout, Nigel will nod, and make the occasional joke. It feels like we've won the war, and that's it. We've shown this town that it has something valuable, like the discovery of a thermal spring that was hidden all along. I'm sure Nigel could pull out a chart and make it seem like it was all a no-brainer. It all comes down to money. Just ask *Birdseye for the Blind*. But it doesn't seem like a victory in the way Nigel thinks it is. If it were a victory, all the townspeople would be happy. It's great to have cash in the bank, but no one lies on their deathbed and remembers all the debt they paid off. If you're an athlete crossing the finish line, you don't punch the air and think about the sponsorship deals. There's no joy in budget surpluses; there's joy in life. This is the best way forward. The romantic way. It leads towards Costa Rica, or the Wordsworth Institute, with daffodils in the front lawn.

I walk for as long as I can while remaining within our settlement. I decide that if I walk any further, they might chase after me. There's no point in getting too attached to our fortress, as it won't exist for much longer.

In the morning the builders will disassemble the pods, put them in a van and drive them to the next town. The kitchen units will be put into storage and used in Sunderland or Dunstable. The litter will be cleared and we'll try to leave the site as we found it (after we've taken pictures for the website). In a more prosperous town, the pod units might be converted into a youth hostel, or temporary art space, but Birdseye isn't there yet.

Ours is the only pod with a light on. My working assumption is that a couple of hours apart will be enough to earn Kendal's forgiveness. I expect she'll be lying on the mattress, staring at the ceiling. If there were a convenience store, I'd buy some flowers and a bottle of wine. I'd make some kind of gesture. It wouldn't be the same to simply grab a beer from the fridge and take it up. I'm convinced of Kendal's unequivocal genius as I climb the stairs and knock on the pod door. I go inside and notice the bed's been made. You can search the whole room in one glance. She's taken her coat from the chair and there aren't any shoes by the door. Her rucksack is gone. I open the drawer and find my folded jumper, which still smells of Kendal. I lift the pillow, which seems futile, even while I'm doing it. I call her mobile and it doesn't even ring. I sit on the bed and realise that I don't even have a television to keep me company. I don't have anything but a small empty room and a beautifully made bed. On the mirror is a taped note. I recognise the handwriting:

Altho' the night were ne'er sae wild,
And I were ne'er sae weary O,
I'll meet thee on the lea-rig,
My ain kind Dearie O.

I peel off the note and my first instinct is to clutch it to my chest. If I hold it tighter, she might come back. And if she doesn't come back, I don't know what I'll do. I try to imagine what she'd want me to do. I can't think of the answer.

They stand around the campfire and project their opinions on sales targets and company socials. In that moment, I feel it wouldn't be a bad thing if everything were swept away. It would be approximately what we deserved.

14

HARIBO MACHT KINDER FROH

'Miles! Time to get ready.'

I find it difficult to summon the strength to rise from my bed. It's hard to get the necessary energy. The pod is the place I'd rather be. I'm happy enough with the dirty worktop and my dirty clothes on the chair. I'm comfortable with my own smell. Out in the cold, they're carrying boxes and starting to load the van. I'm supposed to pack, but I don't feel motivated to fill my suitcase. I want my clothes to stay in the drawer and everything to remain as it is. I want the mugs on the side to wash themselves somehow. On the table is Eden's letter in the envelope. I put it inside my coat pocket and resolve to read it another time. Not today. Today's a bad time. I pull on my coat. I walk down the stairs and immediately catch Nigel's attention.

'Miles! The coach will be here in ten.' I tell him I'm already packed — a lie — and I'm going for a short walk. Nigel seems to ignore the comment and averts his attention to the idle sales team. Everyone seems to holding a paper cup of coffee. 'Come on, guys. Chop, chop!'

The exit day is always complex. We have a good sense of what needs to be done, but little appetite to execute it. We tend to spend most of the time talking about logistics, like who's lifting what and who gets to take the beer home. We don't have to entertain, which means it's fine not to wash, and you can wear whatever you want. Everyone's wearing their worst clothes, the dirty jumpers and jogging bottoms. No one seems to smile as much, because it's no longer a professional obligation. We no longer need to take pictures. We've done a good thing, and we don't need to be told about it anymore. We came, we rebranded, we conquered. History will be our judge, and if historical success is measured by the number of new coffee shops, we will be judged as revolutionaries. Nigel starts to take a register; he's standing with a clipboard and calling names aloud. I walk unnoticed across the rocks and climb the steep verge where I went with Darren. The long road by the shore still doesn't have a coffee shop, but it will. They seem to have started work on converting the old cinema into a block of flats. I'm reminded of the maps we created — the shaded section of designated Opportunity Areas slowly coming to life. You could convert the whole street into something else: the buildings are handsome, sturdy Victorian things. In most other towns they would be occupied by patisseries and knitting shops. Then it occurs to me that the beauty of the town is the fact it was planned for another age: the cinemas, wash houses and gentleman's clubs were meant to be filled with people. There was supposed to be a public of sorts. Then it so happened that people didn't want to live here anymore. Their factories were closed, their work was rendered useless, and the cinemas and wash houses went into ruin. They became fossils. England's Chicago became England's Detroit. I should see the town one last time. I should see it alone, so I can deal with whatever the locals want to yell at me. It seems fair that I should get abused one last time.

I walk as far as I can before I need to eat a bacon sandwich. The man in the café prepares it behind the counter. I ask him if he can remove the fat at the edges. He looks at me like I've forgotten something. We stare it out. I take the silence as an act of contempt. I don't really mind as long as I get my bacon sandwich. I wait for a bit longer and he starts to trim the fat. It's a great victory. He presses the numbers on the till. The price is there for me to see. We don't need to talk about it.

I walk down the street and wonder where else I can go. The pub is a good shout. I enter the Pig & Thistle, where we nearly got killed. The absence of people makes it look bigger than last time, and even less tasteful in its decor. I hadn't noticed the carpet curling up at the skirting board. There's no one waiting at the bar, and no one to serve me. The only occupied table has two gents looking at a newspaper. One of them points at a story — the other one nods. No one wants to talk to me. It's like I'm carrying a smell, and everyone's too polite to say anything. In the corner, I recognise the barmaid who likes dogs and hates people. She's putting up a poster, which she considers more important than serving Miles Platting, language killer. I expect her to say 'I'll be with you in a minute', but all she does is look at me, and tear another piece of tape. She collects four glasses with one hand, using her fingers like a crane grabber to pinch the insides. She doesn't rush her return. I lean across the bar and ask for a shandy, with soda water instead of lemonade.

'It's less calories,' I explain.

She looks at me like I've told her to fuck off. She removes a black marker pen from a drawer and writes the forthcoming football fixtures on a calendar. Then she uses the pen to write me a note:

She doesn't seem to be joking about anything. It seems odd that she's silent, but I put it down to a sore throat.

'Look. I'm leaving Birdseye. I know we didn't get off on the right track . . . ' She looks at me, which is progress, but she doesn't deign to open her mouth. 'I know we're never going to be friends, exactly. But I very much hope your community will be stronger from this experience. Let me tell you, I have a lot of regrets. Nigel thinks it's a passing phase, but I really want to just . . . '

'Shhh,' she says. She points to the red badge pinned to her top: it has a cartoon face and a pursed pair of lips with the words *ZipIt*. She points to a sheet of paper pinned to the toilet door. In printed black text it says:

This is a silent pub. Conversations will not be tolerated.

She's smiling now. I must look pale. She seems excited by the idea that I might look like this for ever. If I always looked like a petrified stone statue, she'd be happy. She waves a hand to say cheerio, and walks into the kitchen.

Someone is clanging a bell. The market

stalls are open, but none of the stallholders say a thing; they communicate with their hands, making numbers with their fingers and thumbs. They exchange a bow with each customer when the purchase has been made. I look at the next man who walks past and he's got a red badge stuck on his jacket which says *#ZipIt*. It's not a day of national remembrance. I haven't disturbed a minute's silence. I want someone to break their stride, turn towards me and say 'Actually mate, this is the revolution'. It would at least explain things somewhat. No one is forthcoming; no one offers an explanation. The town has changed without our approval — it has conjured a system. Charity collectors wave their clipboards; homeless beggars hold 'spare change' signs. The street cleaners with bins-on-wheels seem to carry on without saying anything, although they probably do this every day. A couple of police officers are standing on the pavement, covering their mouths while they talk. Even here, the officers' eyes are alert to the possibility they might be offending someone. And it seems that if they were to break the silence, they'd immediately know what the public think about it. A lollipop man guides a group of schoolchildren across the road; they walk in silence. You can hear them tread on the pavement stones. You can hear the rustle of bags and the ringing of mobile phones unanswered. Some of the children take pleasure in shouting words aloud, but they're shushed by the adults, who tell them not to spoil it. The sounds of street life have intensified: the ignition of car engines, the shopkeepers pulling down shutters, the ambulance siren, the church bell, the cries of birds, slow-moving traffic and exhaust pipe splutter — all of it exists in its own space and of its own accord.

The town crier shakes his bell.

It seems like half the town have a smile on their face. They walk around like extras on a film shoot, satisfied they're doing a great job. No one has ever felt so much a part of something. No one quite knows what to do. No one knows what to make of it all, except to smile and participate. Keep going, keep smiling and think of a strategy later. It's a coordinated effort in so far as the will is there — the will to be a part of something. The fact that no one can speak makes it all the more exciting. The silence is deafening! The silence makes them reflect and look within. People are smiling because they want to say something but know they can't. This is the commitment — a pledge — shared by all. No one wants to disrupt the silence. It seems to be a matter of principle to keep it going. It's a novelty, no doubt, but it might develop into something more. I look at the townspeople and I can't prevent myself from smiling. Kendal will know what's happening. Kendal will like it a lot.

I start to run. With the guide of the clock tower, I run in the direction of the unit base. I run off the bacon sandwich. It's important just to run. Nigel would want to know what's happening.

An old lady stops me and says, 'Have you seen?' She allows a smile to emerge. It's supposed to be a smile, but she hasn't had the practice. 'Absolutely brilliant,' she says. I mention how everyone's wearing a badge. 'Aye.' Her eyes return to their natural state — suspicion — and she walks onwards. 'It's the best way to stick it to 'em. Cos you know they won't bloody listen. No one bloody listens.'

★ ★ ★

We can account for most disasters. Most of the time, there are procedures in place to mitigate any damage. We know about smashed windows, mortar bombs and threats from above. We know about chemicals in the mail and assassination plots — sophisticated or otherwise. We know that anger is a by-product of restlessness. We can ordinarily placate the anger with glass-and-steel shopping centres. In this particular situation, we can't really account for anything. The strength of the protest is determined by the will of the participants. It's an act of silent fury, a revolution without a dent of damage. I run along the shore and I think about whether we're moments away from police cordons and rolling news cameras. Perhaps it's coming.

The way I stumble through the gate makes it look like I've just been attacked in the street. I start shouting long in advance of actually getting close to anyone. I make a big effort to get everyone's attention when their priority is to lift their bags and get on the coach. Someone asks me what's wrong. It gives me the license to announce what needs to be said.

'They're completely silent. They're not saying a fucking thing!'

They gather round, uncertain of what to make of their sweaty, paranoid boss. They seem more concerned for my well-being than for the implications of what I'm saying. I wouldn't be surprised if they brought me a hot flannel. I can see their reluctance to believe it. Aside from my flailing arms, the sweat on my forehead is the only indicator of someone who's telling the truth.

Nigel appears — the frowning headmaster, annoyed with the disturbance at the school gate. 'Miles, what's all this? What's the matter with you?'

'We're under attack.'

'Who's under attack? Where?' He seems to be processing all the reasons why I might be acting this way. Am I on drugs? Am I having a nervous breakdown? He doesn't know what to make of it.

'It's true,' says a member of the tech team, his laptop resting on a rock. He scrolls down the webpage. 'They've got a website. *ZipIt*.' They've published a news item on a temporary landing page which reads:

A silent success — more to follow.

We stand over the computer in silence, as if we're participating in the campaign ourselves. The first order of duty is to instruct the coach driver to turn off the engine. The security convoy is given notice of a delay. Nigel tells Darren to raise the tent so the tech team can work under shelter. He asks the PR manager to call the sponsors and reaffirm our commitment to loud noises.

Another message comes shortly afterwards.

It claims the fight will continue until Birdseye has been renamed Barrow-in-Furness. This is just the beginning, it says.

The English language is nobody's special property. It is the property of the imagination: it is the property of the language itself.

The worst thing is the audacity of it all. It's not so much that they've retaliated — we expected that — but that they've come up with something better than Lingua Franca itself. Darren ties down the tent and announces that it's ready. The tech team — positioned behind their dual computer screens — seem to enjoy the sudden interest in their activities. It suddenly becomes important to dote on them — to ask them technical questions and get them a coffee. They soon establish the direct whereabouts of the enemy — the IP address suggests the messages are coming from the Pig & Thistle, Birdseye. Nigel declares that everything will be fine and that it will only be a passing fad. He says he will reveal a plan of action later. He just needs a little time to think. Until then we should retrieve the table tennis table from the van and try not to panic. Then he takes me aside and asks for the real debrief, like a president consulting his military general at the outbreak of war.

Later on, Nigel takes me to what he calls *the situation room*, a nod to where American presidents conduct their most important operations. It's the largest of the unit pods, and scheduled to remain intact beyond our stay. Nigel opens his laptop and immediately clicks to hide a webpage which displays a naked woman. It makes me sad to think of Nigel as a lonely, childless man, obsessed with work. He manages to maintain a serious face.

'Miles, listen carefully. I need you with me on this one. We've just got to pull together.' He says he will be rolling up his sleeves and working on the 'cold face', by which he means 'coal face'. We talk about what I saw, and whether I could have stopped it. He agrees that I couldn't have done much except to make a note of everything. He seems to sigh every few seconds. He needs more thinking time. 'Here's the thing,' he says, without identifying the thing itself. He makes himself pause. It's Nigel's method of working out the plans in his head. He wants to know he's happy with his own thoughts before sharing them with the world. 'We don't want to make a big fuss. If we make a big noise, the press will get on it. We need to infiltrate them

— silently. We need to play them at their own game.' Then he proceeds to move the nearest object — a red beaker, as it turns out — to one side of the table. 'This is us,' he says of the beaker, 'and this is them,' he partners it with a stapler. He starts moving the beaker and stapler around the table, exchanging their positions as he talks. 'We have the ability to infiltrate them from two crossings,' he explains, using a blunt pencil to signify the Walney Channel. To the west is the Walney Bridge, the normal route, or 'decoy'. To the south-east is the narrow basin leading to the Buccleuch Dock — soon to be the Birdseye Dock — allowing direct access to the heart of the town. 'We just need to find a way of gaining access.' He enjoys the urgency of the situation. He's most alive when there's a crisis to manage. My job is to listen, and validate what he says. I try to act like I'm angry too. I try to reflect the gravity of the situation through my facial expressions. I try not to smile. He probably thinks I'm a *quisling*. Nigel taps his pen on the desk. He can't get rid of his frown. 'Leave it with me,' he says, which is code for 'go away'. Then he gets up from his chair — he needs the space to walk around. 'I think we can do it. We can outfox them.' The purpose of the meeting has been met. He says he will make an announcement in a couple of hours. 'Meeting adjourned.'

⋆ ⋆ ⋆

The tent can't fit more than five or six, which doesn't stop the surge. 'Look here,' the web manager says, pointing at the screen. There's another post on the *ZipIt* website.

> *Kindness is the language that the deaf can hear and the blind can see.*

No one has very much to say. A couple of journalists have begun to gather at the barrier; the world wants to know what's happening. In their frustration, the team sit around the luggage, hoping we might be ready to go soon, and texting friends and family to rearrange plans. The atmosphere changes. There's a thinly disguised annoyance that Nigel has yet to formalise a plan. It goes from a situation where everyone was looking forward to going home, to anxiety that no one knows when that might be. Our objective is for Birdseye to fall in love with Lingua Franca, but Lingua Franca seems to be falling out of love with itself. All the while, Nigel arranges the logistics. He gets on the phone to a catering company and asks for a quote on two crates of non-perishables. He speaks to a wholesaler in the hope of getting cheap energy drinks. He speaks to Birdseye, who want an update on the situation. They don't express an opinion one way or another — they just want an update.

The announcement comes in the evening that, yes, we will be staying at the unit base in an attempt to secure the town. Nigel says it's an emergency measure and not one he takes lightly. As for *ZipIt*, Nigel describes it as a fad — a momentary spell in which most of the townspeople have lost their senses. It would be foolish to assume it was anything more than that. The staff are roughly divided into two groups: those who are annoyed at having to stay, and those who seek to make themselves useful. In the latter camp, the tech team are the busiest. It seems like every five minutes *ZipIt* posts a new bulletin on the theme of silence.

If you've ever visited the Sistine chapel, you'll know how much nicer it would be if everyone would shut the fuck up.

In only a few hours, *ZipIt* attract thousands of social media followers. They upload images of children pursing their lips, and a *#ZipIt* flag unfurled outside the Pig & Thistle.

There's talk of making it a nationwide campaign of silence. In the scheduled programme of events, there's a *silent fest* earmarked for 2pm the next day. We spend a moment debating what exactly's meant by a silent fest. Nigel is informed just in case it alters his plans for the offensive (it does). He then announces that he needs a bit more time to think; he relays the news like an airport official announcing a delay; in turn, the passengers groan. Nigel says that everything will be resolved soon. The energy drinks are coming. Further details will be announced in due course.

Dinner consists of marshmallows and biscuits. There's a sense that we won't know the plan until the morning, when Nigel will burst from his pod and shout, 'I've got it!' Some of the team sit around a fire. Most of the agitators talk in the abstract about how Lingua Franca has let down its staff. Some of them try to recall details of their contracts in which it might have said something about unsociable hours. Nobody's certain. They don't seem to mind that I'm sitting among them; in fact, they say I'm much better than Nigel and that everything would be fine if I was solely in charge. One of them sarcastically says, 'We love you, Miles!'

I do my best to put on a diplomatic company voice. I say, 'Come on now, Nigel's a busy man.'

They seem to understand that I don't believe what I'm saying. They know I'm doing a corporate bluff, that I need to say this to protect the firm and to kid myself into believing I'm not wasting my life. They have figured me out, as we look at the fire and do our own silent thing. Darren asks if I think Kendal's involved in the protest. I squeeze a marshmallow onto the end of a fork and say, 'Probably, mate.' Then Darren asks if I want to drink in the pub. I tell him we probably shouldn't. No one knows what's going to happen, and who knows, we might be killed.

Nigel's light is on. We watch the balcony from which he might emerge. He seems to have momentarily forgotten we exist. I can imagine him sitting at his desk with his battle map, working out the coordinates. He will have got himself into a rapture, caught in the excitement of being Field Marshal Haig. Some time later, he steps out of his room and asks why we're still awake. He tells us to get some sleep, as tomorrow's a big day. 'Tomorrow we'll hit 'em hard.'

★ ★ ★

At quarter to nine the next morning there's still a queue for the showers. Some of the team decide to give up and tolerate their own smell. There's a feeling of dread when everyone enters the meeting room. It would have made sense — politically at least — for Nigel to prepare coffee and sandwiches for us all. That would have helped quell the anger.

'Thanks for your patience,' Nigel announces to the room. He has the look of a man who seems certain of what he's doing. A frightening thought. 'I know this has been a difficult twenty-four hours. Ladies and gentlemen, our objective is simple. We will protect our brand, whatever the cost may be. We will protect our livelihood and liberate Birdseye from the rule of the mob.' We will be carrying out an operation that — if successful — will enable us to depart within a matter of hours, he says. We will follow an intervention-ist strategy, designed to prevent further conflict. The uprising will be halted; order will be restored. All it requires is one swift effort. 'Listen carefully, comrades. I only have to explain this once.' The strategy is two-fold. A team of staff — he hesitates to say troops — will arrive by foot via the Walney Bridge. The other half will arrive by boat, making a back-door arrival through the Port of Barrow while the enemy is distracted. The aim will be to infiltrate different parts of the town and to talk aloud so that normality is restored. We will position ourselves in cafés and pubs, on the high street and in the middle of the town square. It will be infectious, creating a knock-on effect that will inspire others to talk again. It will be a spectacle of our own. 'Ladies and gentlemen, the cost of inaction far exceeds the cost of action. We don't want this incident to light the blue touch paper. We want to douse the flames.'

Most people in the room don't want to hear about formations and pincer movements — they want tea and toast. So it's not a surprise that when Nigel says, 'Any questions?' the only response concerns the whereabouts of their breakfast. Nigel confirms that supplies will be arriving within the hour, and that we'll all be fed in advance of our voyage. Then in a bid to pretend his speech contains the requisite momentum, he raises a fist and shouts: 'Onwards!'

We exit the meeting room and no one knows what to say. On the edge of the waterline are a variety of small vessels, fishing boats, pedalos, speedboats and pleasure craft. It's a shame for Nigel that he couldn't procure ground-to-air missiles. He shakes hands with a man who's pulling a motor boat ashore. Nigel promises we'll return the boats within two hours and without a hint of damage.

'Gather round, everyone.' Nigel isn't literally rolling up his sleeves, but it's the image he would most like to convey. He asks us to form a line so he can put us into groups. 'These are the vessels that will help win the peace. Those of you travelling by foot should depart within five minutes. Those of you travelling by sea should follow the motor boat until we reach the Port of Barrow, then disembark. In the meantime, please help yourselves to some crisps. There's beer in the fridge for our celebration tonight.'

He says that now's the best time to use the bathroom. It might be a long wait until there's another chance to go. We look at each other. If anyone's going to object, now would be the time. Ninety per cent of the staff will do what they're told, whatever it entails. Nigel could lead them on a military coup and most of them would oblige. I look at the agitators, who seem unimpressed, but silent. There aren't many reasons to go, but not many reasons to stay. Darren takes a knife to a cardboard box and carves it open. He distributes the crisps. We look at each other and we form a line.

15

THE FIGHTING TEMERAIRE

'So we got a load of boats together and said *bon voyage*!'

No one's listening. Life continues on the ward, if 'life' means the temporary suspension of death. I've tried to narrate as best as I can, in spoken words for the most part, but sometimes on paper. Still, no one listens. They never reply when I speak aloud. They'd rather pretend I don't exist.

Gerry, the white-haired male patient nearest to the door, is sitting upright in bed with a bowl of cherries. The nurse places a coffee and an out-of-date *Telegraph* on his bedside. The nurse knows all the moves: how to pour tea in the cup, and when to smile at all the patients except me. She plumps up Gerry's pillow so he can rest his head. I look more alive than Gerry. I don't know what Gerry does for a living: at a guess, I'd say *fisherman*. He just has a fisherman vibe. I can imagine him throwing a net into the ocean and reeling in hundreds of cod. I can imagine him sitting in a fisherman's cottage listening to 'When the Ship Comes In', the Bob Dylan song. Here's to Gerry. I don't feel the same ache in my shoulder as I did before. My rib doesn't have that sharp pain when I touch it with my little finger. I don't feel ill, other than when they tell me I am. Even when you look at the other patients, none of them appear to have any physical pain. They seem tired, and mute, but not exactly suffering. The nurse puts a chocolate bar next to Gerry's coffee. Is this fair? Maybe he's about to die and it's his last meal. I wonder if they'd treat me nicely if they thought I was about to die. I decide not to make a thing of it and instead focus on writing my apology note. I take out a fresh sheet and lean closer:

Sorry for my behaviour last night.
Best wishes, Miles.

I seal it in an envelope. Once the nurse has propped up Gerry's feet, I raise my hand to get her attention. I pass her the note. She opens it and reads without changing her expression. She takes a pen and does a tick next to my words, like she's a teacher. She just puts *OK*, which means we're okay. She looks at her watch and exits the room. I look at Gerry, who closes his eyes and leans back against the headboard. He's seemingly unaware of the newspaper and the chocolate. If he is aware, it's only because he considers it normal to be in receipt of gifts.

'Hey, Gerry!' He doesn't even open his eyes. 'Gerry! I know you can hear me. She's gone, Gerry. What did you do to get in her good books, eh? It's just yak-yak-yak with you, Gerry, isn't it? I can't get a word in edgeways. What's the deal with you, anyway? Hello?'

He opens his eyes and says, 'Huh?' like he's woken up from a bad dream and doesn't know where he is. He looks at me and starts to stutter. 'D-d-d-duh, duh . . . '

'What's up?'

He tries to talk but it's like he's swallowed cement. I've never seen him like this. 'D-d-d-do . . . do as they say.' He grabs hold of his bed sheets as though he were strapped to a roller coaster. 'It . . . it . . . it's the only way out.'

The door opens and the nurse enters with a hot-water bottle. She notices a change in Gerry's expression. She puts a hand on his forehead. She looks at Gerry and signs a gesture. Gerry nods in reply.

'Is he alright?'

The nurse pulls the curtain across Gerry. She writes a note and shoves it in my hand.

He's got a big day today. Let him rest.

213

'He doesn't look well. And he said something weird.'

He's getting better. Now tell me how the story ends.

★ ★ ★

The operation has a code name: Barbara. As if it were a hurricane. We move in an arrow, broadly speaking, with Nigel's boat at the tip. We do well to navigate the channel, moving a safe distance from the trawlers and ferry ships. The flotilla demonstrates our unity and strength. It's a spectacle, an extraordinary sight. There's a hierarchy of sorts. The best boat belongs to the operations team, a white motor boat with a small deck for sitting. One of the sailing boats seems the most fun — they have an acoustic guitar and sing songs about wanting to go home. The most junior staff sit in the pedalos, bobbing along the Port of Barrow in their ladybirds and swans. The hardest part is navigating the left turn into the Buccleuch Dock, which enables our back door passage. Ours is probably the calmest boat, owing to the fact I'm accompanied by Darren, who takes responsibility for steering. I only have to concern myself with dragging the oars through the water.

Darren looks at the sea like it's deliberately trying to annoy him. 'This is long.' He says he misses working for his dad's building company and he'd rather be knocking through kitchen walls than protecting a branding consultant from certain death. 'I can't be arsed with this anymore. I'm gonna go into electrics, man. Get my Part P.'

'Can you keep me alive in the meantime?'

'Yeah, mate. But then I'm quitting.'

'You won't.'

'One hundred per cent.'

'But you always say this. And you never quit.' I say this because it's true. Darren's a guy who will be loyal to the regime until the end. There could be a massive earthquake and he'd still stick to whatever task he's doing.

'Yeah, well . . . ' Darren gives the sea a dirty look. 'This is long . . . '

I thank Darren for keeping me alive all this time. If we had any beer, we'd clink glasses in solidarity. But if we had beer, we'd probably sink the boat.

We keep track of the flotilla and say nothing for a bit. Darren shakes his head. 'Eden, man . . . '

'What about him?'

He looks at the sea, and for a moment he

215

forgives the ocean. 'I'm reading Lance Armstrong's book. That man had mental strength. He had cancer and he never gave up. He won the Tour de France seven times.'

'Didn't he get caught doping?'

'Where did you hear that?'

I drop it. I want to say something like 'There's nothing wrong with giving up', but I don't think Darren would like to hear it. He clings to the promise of tomorrow — futureness. In any case, I can only think about the office, the crowd gathered at the window and the silence that fell when Eden jumped. I almost forget where we're going and what the objective is. It's only when we notice the other boats turning left that we start moving in the right direction. For many of the team, the voyage is an inconvenience, a major incursion into their after-hours that should never have been authorised. Still, the structure of our formation remains intact, and Barbara is well underway.

The tech team, back at the ranch, appoint themselves as meteorological experts, announcing via mobile phone that we can expect heavy thunder. We can see Nigel gesticulating at the front of his boat. We can imagine the others cursing Nigel and considering whether to turn around. The further we go the more Nigel appears to increase his speed. We go on, driving forward in the rain, and struggle to see the point of our activity any more than we can see through the torrent.

As the docking bay comes into sight, we feel more exposed. Some of the locals watch from above; they seem confused as to what's happening. We're a thing, something to notice. It takes a while for all our boats to assemble. Some of the team hopscotch from boat to boat just to disembark. Nigel pulls us onto the deck. We're reeled in slowly. It takes a moment to get everyone to stand in one place. Nigel instructs us on where to stand; he insists on making everyone form a line. There's an order to proceedings. He passes around maps which outline the supermarkets, cafés and squares where each talker should stand and speak. The conversations needn't be about anything in particular — the most important thing is that they talk aloud. They can speak about anything as long as it's disruptive.

'This is a bloodless revolution,' Nigel says. 'Lingua Franca will live on. Our language shall not perish from the earth.'

'Do we get umbrellas?' someone asks.

'Of course you don't.'

There's laughter, which spoils the mood Nigel was hoping to establish. He forces a smile, but in reality he wants to court martial them all. We're supposed to have the makings of a professional army, not an army of Mary Poppinses.

We target the supermarket because it's supposed to be a business-friendly zone, a privately run enterprise that's sympathetic to our needs to make money. We probably arouse their suspicions as soon as we enter. At first it doesn't seem so different from any other supermarket. The noise is what you'd find in any shopping environment — beeping checkouts, moving trolleys and public announcements. No one seems to be talking; they seem more focused on pulling items from the shelves. Nigel approaches a member of staff and asks for the time. The shop assistant makes a shushing gesture and points to the red *#ZipIt* badge on his shirt. The logo has design agency production values — a cartoon face with a zip in place of lips. It has been made by clever people with design software and an eye for colour. It's easily replicable and indeed, appears at the front of each aisle, on shelves, on display signs, T-shirts and stickers. There's even a sign at the checkout which reads:

Proud to be supporting #ZipIt.

The whole thing seems to unsettle Nigel. What hurts him is that our own brand of cynicism has been met by theirs: the supermarket feigns compassion for the community, and makes accommodations for silence. It's a localised marketing strategy, in much the same way a fast-food chain might serve halal hamburgers. Nigel takes a moment to think. Then he moves from one team member to the next, tapping each on the shoulder. One at a time, we disperse down separate aisles. Nigel does his best attempt at a purposeful stride. As soon as the first words leave our mouths, we've alerted them. We've disrupted their peace. It doesn't take long before the whole group — just under twenty — are speaking aloud all at once. We find that we're free to talk uninhibited. We talk about nothing of any consequence — a mad clatter of words. The sentences are disordered — a mangled syntax detached from meaning. Eventually it gathers a rhythm, a spontaneity. Some of the elderly folks turn to look at us, which feels like a victory. The danger comes from our own complacency. The fact we're unobstructed means we run out of things to say: we end up repeating ourselves. Some of the talkers smile at one another, as though the whole thing's a joke. Nigel frowns at them and they soon get back to their babble. Nigel becomes more relaxed; he enjoys what he sees and he looks like he's going to steal a beer from the fridge. He's buoyed by the lack of retaliation. He has the confidence to point in whichever direction he thinks people should be moving; he's guiding the traffic. Some of the locals frown at the talkers as if they've interrupted the eleventh hour of the eleventh day of the eleventh month. There's a loud siren that rings out across the whole supermarket. It means the guards start to shout for everyone to exit. The customers aren't happy at having to leave their half-emptied trolleys at the checkout. Some try to leave the exact change at the scanners, which become improvised honesty trays. The guards attempt to usher everyone through the doors. It seems like the whole place is beginning to empty. Suddenly we're outside, unsure of how to locate each other; we're drunk nightclub revellers who can't find our friends.

'Forward!' is the shout from Nigel.

For the first time, we seem united. We're joined by the decoy team, who came from the west and report no interference. We can move as we please, without having to plan a trajectory. We talk as loud as we want. Nigel smiles. It feels like the first stages of a victory. We've stormed the gates and now we're marching on the palace: the gates are automatic supermarket doors and the palace is a WHSmith. We walk a few hundred feet; we open our mouths and speak with greater certainty than before. The sign at the top of the high street says:

You are now entering a Quiet Zone.
Please respect our way of life.

Our route takes us via the posters and billboards from the day of our launch. It seems like half the town is penned off with 'site acquired' signs, each displaying a champagne and canapés lifestyle. Investment is coming, and investment means well-dressed models you can touch on a billboard. It means pubs selling pints out of jam jars; novelty cafés selling nothing but cereal and marina apartments for absentee landlords. No more butchers, bakers and candlestick makers, unless in an ironic context. *Vive la révolution!* We walk as far as a parade of shops, at which point Nigel shouts, 'Stop!' He wants to strategise. He encourages us to stand in a circle like it's an *expression session.*

'We've come this far, ladies and gentlemen. Keep walking, and if you can't think of anything to say, just make up some football scores. Now's the time to strike!' Everyone cheers. The vibe is somewhere between a paintball session on a company jolly and a historical re-enactment of an Arthurian legend. Nigel split us into twos and threes. He points at where he wants us to go: the pub for some, and the betting shops, cafés and high street for the rest.

We walk forward and I'm accompanied by Darren, who looks alert, keeping his eye out for rattlesnakes. 'Manchester United two . . . Queens Park Rangers one.'

The path in front of us is clear. We're faced with an empty town square and a free space in which to move. 'Aston Villa three . . . Sheffield Wednesday one.' The localisation team enter the bakery. 'Crystal Palace two . . . Arsenal three.' The sales team surround the pound shop. 'Plymouth Argyle nil . . . Leyton Orient one.'

From the distance comes the beat of a drum. It sounds in three thuds, followed by a pause, then three thuds again. We can hear the drum getting louder, and footsteps, too. The drum pounds. We turn the corner and we're suddenly met by a herd — one hundred or so townspeople. They move in two rigid banks, the makings of a rugby scrum. They wear *#ZipIt* badges and hold a large banner that says the same thing. Kendal's at the front. She points to the sky, and so does everyone else. They move to the beat and follow Kendal, the mad movement therapist. She's leading a protest without any chanting; it makes us concentrate on the music. There's a military drum roll, trumpeters, brass instruments, acoustic guitars, bells, whistles and maracas. Their music is louder than anything we can conjure. We've stepped into their jungle. They seem to know exactly when to move and how to surround us. Their strength is in their co-ordination — they position themselves the full way across the road, a concave shape that threatens to swallow us whole. We don't want to step near in case we get thwacked by the drumsticks. They have something we don't possess: determination. We have office workers — they have a tribe.

'West Bromwich Albion three!' Nigel shouts. 'Stoke City . . . nil . . . ' The drum continues to pound, building in its rhythm to reflect the ever-growing charge. The natural response is to listen out for Nigel's scores, but he can't be heard. He's trying to say something about Wigan Athletic but no one knows what. There's silence in our ranks. The one-hundred-strong marching band leave us unable to whisper, let alone speak. What they have on us — besides the moral authority

— is the music. They charge, not with thrown fists, but with a rush of intent. We're huddled together, owing to the surge. Those of us who were apart are brought closer together. We're kettled into a corner, squashed between two lamp posts in the pedestrianised strip. We're surrounded; there's no room to sidestep, less chance to run. Some photographers do their best to get into the middle.

'Stay calm!' Nigel shouts. 'Everton two . . . Wycombe Wanderers . . . '

The music starts again. The strength of their numbers forces us back. The retreat is instinctive — it happens because it has to. None of us want to fight. None of us want a broken nose. It's not part of our terms and conditions. Nigel makes an attempt to call the unit base; he holds his phone with two hands and speaks into it like it's a shortwave radio. 'Nigel to unit base . . . can you hear me? Nigel to unit base . . . prepare the docking station. Mission aborted, I repeat . . . mission aborted . . . '

The trumpeters' tune gets more euphoric. We do our best to tread backwards without falling over. We're confident enough that we won't be captured — more like driven out of town. There's an order to our chaos. The brass band seems to enjoy our retreat; the pace of the music quickens with each backward step. Our scampering has its own soundtrack.

Nigel scrambles himself to the docking station. He holds the rope in his hands, ready to let it go. He's always dreamed of being an admiralty officer of some sort. He's used to this scenario, in his head. He waves an arm to make us hurry. He wags a finger at each of us and starts counting aloud. The only option is to embark. Kendal beckons the photographers and gestures for them to take pictures. She knows what the front page headlines will be. Lingua Franca will be famous for being a shambles, incapable of keeping its empire in check. She knows how to bring about our end. Nigel understands this too. Far better to limit the damage than to allow our total destruction.

They watch as we clamber aboard; we no longer recite football scores. They pipe up with their version of 'La Marseillaise', substituting the words for 'da dada', which is permitted. Then we hear a drum roll, which continues until Nigel turns the key on the motor boat engine. The roar is enormous! They hug one another, swing scarves, jump up and down, high five, and in perfect unison, give us a sarcastic cheerio wave. We drift into the sea. Even after a few minutes, we can hear them belt out another chorus.

We're silent, which no doubt would get their approval.

The rain doesn't relent. For a while we can see nothing but grey mist. All we have is our instinct. I keep hold of the oar but the current threatens to take it off me. Darren tries to grip the rudder thing. The wind starts to whistle. We angle our bodies to try and veer the boat in a straight line. Our boat begins to swerve — it rides over waves like they're speed bumps. The wind picks up — it seems to increase our speed by a hundred knots. We ride the waves and the feeling in my stomach is like being in a rising elevator.

'Hold on!'

The storm sweeps us along. We can't move the boat as well as the sea can move us. We can't turn back, but neither does it seem like we can carry on. In the fog, we meet great resistance. A sudden backlift hits the waves and seems to raise us into the clouds. We land on the water and somehow we're spat out into the blue, still sitting in our seats. We traverse the dock and we've settled, it seems. We can see right across the channel.

'Darren? Are you okay, Darren?'

He mumbles that he's okay. He's splayed on the back seat; he looks like someone's thrown a bucket of water over him. He tells me that I'm drenched. I feel secure enough to crawl forward and get a better view. In the distance is a red light which we think is the sun. We want to get to it, whatever it is. Behind us, most of the boats bob along, waterborne. We can see the motor boats and fishing vessels, but none of the pedalos. Nigel will be seasick. In front of us we can see that the red light is a red flare.

'One more push, Darren!' Together we heave, pulling the oars through the water. We're happy to grunt and sweat, which is worth the goal of getting ashore. 'Keep going!'

It gets cold for a second, then it gets darker as we see the shadow descend. If we were sitting at home, this is when the teacups would start to rattle.

'Oh God . . . '

'Keep going!'

'Miles!'

Behind us we can see the curled wave rising. I cling to my knees. We're sitting at a steep angle, and the boat begins to tip. The only blessing is that we don't have time to think. Someone slowly dims the lights.

★   ★   ★

I wake under a mass of splintered wood. At first I think the dampness is blood, but it turns out to be engine oil. I can taste sea salt. The seagulls seem to peck around me, disappointed I'm not a dead rotting carcass. I can twitch my toes but not my legs. Through a gap in the ceiling — or what constitutes a ceiling — I can see the sky. I'm alive. For the moment at least, that's enough.

I shout for some time, calling my own name. 'I'm Miles Platting! I'm here!' I wish I could pull an emergency alarm and wait for more information. I'm alone with the garden gnome and porcelain rabbits. And I realise it makes no difference whether it's called a garden gnome or a rusty spoon. When you're buried underground, words mean nothing: anything can be anything. The broken pipe is a piano. The metal bolt is a giraffe. I just need to find a tortoise and dig my way out of this milkshake.

I have time to think, which means I think about Kendal. I decide that raging married couples should just trap themselves under-ground. No need for therapy. All you need is rocks and darkness. I think about Kendal's approach to the search-and-rescue mission. She'd look through her binoculars in case I'm clinging to a buoy. She'd inform the officials that I don't like getting my toes wet. She'd find me, somehow, and I'd ask whether there's still time to visit Costa Rica, and make another world, or something.

★ ★ ★

'And then you guys rescued me.'

The nurse continues to pace around. I thought she would be sitting round my bedside, gripped by the details of my story. She doesn't seem to care very much. The patients are just as silent as they've ever been. It's no use trying to talk them out of it. I click the cap onto the pen. I relax into my lying position and close my eyes. I resolve to let sleep do its thing, and we can see what happens next.

I can hear them scribbling something onto paper. The grey squirrel compares two different clipboards. Gerry's eyes are closed and his mouth is agape. If he's dead, no one seems very worried about it. I recognise the security guard, who mouths something to the doctor. Together, they lift Gerry by his arms and hoist him to his feet. Gerry doesn't seem to mind. He lets them adjust his body position and turn him towards the door. It's like it's a familiar routine, and he's going for his weekly beard trim. They look pleased with him. Whatever he's done, he's done a good thing. They pull his arms into a red robe. They adjust his collar and tighten his belt.

They check to make sure his sandals are fixed tight to his feet. They spin him around to ensure his legs and waist are fully covered. Then they upturn his palm and place a candle in his grip. It's like he's being prepared for his own funeral. They look at me and offer no explanation. If I ask what's happening, they'll stare at me like I'm stupid. The guard opens the door and I watch them lead Gerry on the start of his procession. The other patients get on with the business of keeping their eyes closed. None of them seem to care, which makes me doubt myself for a moment. It's like I'm in a dream, but somehow I've seen this before. I've seen the robed men, the candlelit path and night-time cinema screenings. I've seen it, and I want to know what's going on. I want a bowl of cherries and unexplained chocolate. I want a hot-water bottle and a copy of something (not the *Telegraph*). I want to be told I'm doing well, and I want to be robed. I want to know where Darren and Nigel and Kendal have gone, what their story is, and how it's going to end.

16

BANANA REPUBLIC

The plan is to do nothing and think of nothing. The good thing about a self-imposed coma is that it removes you from responsibility. If someone were to call my name, I wouldn't have to say anything. I transfer all my energy into thinking about Kendal, and whether we'll ever be reunited. I think about Costa Rica, the Wordsworth Institute and whether she'll be sitting at home with a blueprint. You would think the nurses would pass me a phone — mine's out of battery — and put Kendal on the line, with special dispensation to talk. You would think I might have heard from Nigel or the tech team. Perhaps the hospital has strict confidentiality procedures, and doesn't disclose details of each patient until it deems it necessary. It's possible that Lingua Franca has been destroyed, that no one made it back ashore, that the tech team will have been washed away. I think about logistics, like who's going to reset the out-of-office emails, and who's taking the *expression sessions*. I think about our clients, and whether they know I'm lying in a hospital bed in the outskirts of Birdseye-in-Furness. I think about these things and it makes me frown. I'm excited, though, by the prospect of doing nothing, and seeing where that gets me. I look at the ceiling and then the window. I can see a tree blowing in the wind; for once, the sky has decided to be blue. I look at the clock on the wall and it occurs to me that time doesn't matter very much. I get into a relaxed state. The muscles in my legs have begun to soften. I'm perfectly still, a fallen tree trunk. It doesn't seem to matter that I don't have any books to read or programmes to watch. I like the sound of my own silence. I lie with a straight back. The ache in my shoulder has gone, and I don't have any pain in my legs. Even the bruising on my arm is starting to heal. If anything, I want to get up. I ought to ride a bicycle, or go fell running in the Cumbrian mist. I get a look from the nurse, but I don't bother to engage. Better to stay silent. I should get a sign to drape around my neck: *please knock before disturbing*.

What will the historians say about Lingua Franca? Perhaps someone will continue our life's work, and complete the task of renaming every town until nothing's left but Middlesbrough. No one wants Middlesbrough. They'll associate us with tragedy, and name towns in our honour. They'll name a boulevard after Darren, and a swamp after Nigel. They'll name a bridge after Eden, near where he fell. They should put a plaque on the paving stones where he used to walk to the station. He should be referred to in the local history books as an agitator, someone who couldn't bring down the system, so brought down himself. They should preserve his letter in the National Archives, provided I come across well. Perhaps I'll be immortalised through legend. Chipping Norton will be renamed Miles Platting. This train terminates at Miles Platting, change here for local bus services to Miles Platting International Airport. I'll be revered as a pioneer of change, or hated as an agent of destruction, depending on the whims of the moment. I could always make a deathbed conversion, and renounce my throne. Kendal would be proud.

The nurse is tending to the patient opposite, a young male whose leg is suspended in a cast. In all this time, he's not displayed anything resembling a personality; he's been silent on the subject of everything. He's spent a long time reading books like *The Spirit Level*. Behind the silence, he's a thinking creature. To someone who doesn't understand his culture, his long, curly haircut invites prejudice from those who'd call him a hipster or a hippie. He's happy enough to sit and read his books, occasionally pressing the bell and writing a message to request some water. He seems to approve of the salads they serve, and the only thing you could say for certain is that he doesn't want to talk. The nurse looks at him. She opens a small bag of candles and hands one to the doctor. The security guard emerges and it happens again; they lift the patient to his feet, put his arms in a robe, place a candle in his palm and walk him towards the door. He looks glad. It's like he's finally being allowed to board a flight after a long delay. I rise to my feet and immediately become the focus of the nurse's attention. She thinks I'm going to run, or do something wild. I make a toilet gesture, the shoulder tap, and she lets me proceed. I walk to the gents and lock myself inside the cubicle. I open the misted window and watch the robed patient exit the building and walk along the path, accompanied by the security guard. They walk at a slow pace like they're in a carnival procession and the public need a moment to take pictures. The patient doesn't look like he's going to run anywhere. By the way he walks, he seems pretty happy about the whole thing. In the other direction, another robed patient passes them and nods. If I stand for much longer, I'll arouse the suspicions of the nurse, who doesn't want me to do anything unusual, ever. I walk back to my bay and ignore the nurse, who seems glad at my return to bed-stricken normality. I lie back and do the whole silent thing again. I close my eyes and sense that my body needs to shut down. I'm lying in a hospital bay with two empty beds and nothing to do. I'm conscious that I'm smothered in my own words, the countless notes and letters I've written, most of which have been ignored (until the National Archives obtains them). I put a hand to my forehead and I seem to sigh by instinct. The nurse puts a glass of water by my bedside. I sit upright and some of the paper sheets flutter onto the floor. The nurse lifts one of the sheets, leans on the window ledge and writes something. She gives me a sheet and there's another tick.

You've been better this morning. Keep it up.

★   ★   ★

She opens a drawer and puts a bag of sweets by my side. I want to say thank you, and strike a conciliatory note, but it's hard when you're not allowed to speak. I don't know why she's being nice. I might be getting prepped for being told something terrible.

235

This might be the Mental Resistance Unit, where you're prepared for the terrible news that's about to follow. They'll lead us to a room where we bear witness to a tragedy. Everyone's gone, Miles. They drowned at sea. You're the last survivor. Please accept the recovered property we've collected from the shore: Nigel's briefcase and Darren's video game console. I'll take it all home in a van and cry into my pillow while Ptolemy eats my hair.

The nurse refers to her clipboard, looks into my eyes and makes a couple of notes. I've done a good thing. I'm not sure what I've done, but it's good I've done it. I should keep it up.

★ ★ ★

The days pass, and they continue to say I'm doing a good job. They seem determined to praise me incessantly for doing nothing. They make notes on a clipboard and they tell me I'm getting better. They smile at everything. On every sheet of paper, I get a tick. If they gave out red stickers, I'd be covered in them. They respond to my requests — all handwritten — with an unfailing courtesy. They're apologetic when they're being too slow. They seem glad to bring me pens, and they always ensure there's enough paper in case I want to write something. They serve me salad and top up my water; they plump up the pillow and pull down the retractable TV. They bring me trays of tea with lots of different options: camomile . . . Earl Grey . . . They insist I can't do without a hot-water bottle (and I agree). The only time they show any disapproval is when I laugh at a joke on the TV. It's not a problem if I laugh, so long as I don't accompany it with actual words.

I start pressing the bell with a greater frequency. I press it when the temperature's too cold, and when I want water. I make no apologies for wanting a better duvet, and it doesn't seem rude to ask if they can put on the football. The one thing they don't have is a phone charger, which means I'm unable to contact the outside world. I can only presume that text messaging is permitted under the silent state.

The nurse approaches with a catering tray and silver dome. Even when she's at her smiliest, a small part of me worries she'll pull out a gun. She lifts the lid to reveal a selection of cheeses: Stilton . . . Brie . . . and BT Sport, formerly Wensleydale. The nurse cuts a bunch of grapes at the stem and puts them on the plate. Then she removes a corkscrew from a drawer and grimaces as she opens a bottle of

Gazprom. I smile in order to show my gratitude. I raise my glass as if to say *cheers*. If Kendal were here, she'd flick my forehead and say, 'You idiot! You hated them a few days ago.' I would point out to Kendal that no one's offering her any cheese, so it's easy for her to say what she likes. I would cite this as a major flaw in her argument. The nurse watches me cut the BT Sport. She makes a sign gesture, which I take to mean *how is it?* It's good, but it tastes more like Barclays. I nod and raise my thumb. She smiles and writes, *Well done, Miles*. She leaves the room. I make a gurgle at the back of my throat, just to check my vocal chords are still functional. I avoid saying anything in words; if she overheard me, she'd confiscate my cheese and I'd have to start all over. It's like I'm playing a wire buzzer game where you've got to move around the circuit with a steady hand. One small mistake will send me back to the beginning.

★ ★ ★

I lie in my bed and await my morning coffee, which is supposed to arrive at nine. No one's brought my out-of-date copy of *The Guardian*, let alone a croissant. I might have offended them, or I might have entered a new phase: a weaning phase, where I'm deprived of food and drink to teach me a lesson. I press the bell and no one comes. Should I make a complaint if it gets to twenty-past and there's no sign of coffee? I set my expression to a frown: a solid frown from which I don't intend to relax. There's a noise in the hallway, a man shouting. I can see the guard attempting to pull him along. It's like he's pulling a piano and sizing up how to get it through the door. There's a momentary struggle and finally the man is relinquished. I know the face. His arm is in a sling and someone needs to straighten his blue patient gown. His lip seems to be healing from a cut. But still, I know the face.

'Miles!' You could read Nigel's expression a number of ways. He simultaneously looks happy I'm alive, angry I didn't call him and confused by the whole thing. He doesn't seem to know what to think, or which emotion is best. 'Thank God! We need to shut these people down. These people are animals, Miles.'

The nurse looks alarmed that we appear to know each other. There's been a mistake, a glitch in the system. The nurse unfolds the duvet so that Nigel might lie down. He remains standing. He wags a finger in their direction. 'Have you heard of the NHS constitution? This is an abdication of your responsibilities!'

They shush him when he speaks. He raises a finger and says, 'I will not be silenced!' They look at one another like it's time to activate the emergency procedure. Some kind of chokehold, no doubt. Nigel looks at me like he's a Shakespearean messenger; he has some important information and he needs to let it be known. 'Miles, these people are criminals. They don't know the first thing about running a hospital. They refuse to let me speak and they won't let me make any calls.' He rages about the lack of Wi-Fi, and the inherent bias in giving some patients coffee and cake.

I keep my arms at my side.

'Miles? Are you listening? I can't get hold of anyone. Where's Darren? And Kendal? I got lost in the storm until I got dragged out by these savages. Miles? Say something!' He points at me and shouts to the room, 'This man is under duress! Is there a lawyer in the house?' The guard creeps towards him like he's trying to catch a mouse. 'This is a violation of every conceivable UN charter!' I've never seen him wail so much. The guard closes in on the mouse and grabs hold of him. 'Let go of me! What is this?' The nurse beckons for another guard. They grapple until the guards begin to dominate. 'Miles! Get them off me! We can take them! Miles!' The nurse looks at me, making sure I realise there will be consequences if I help. I look at the ceiling and say nothing, like a good silent citizen. I keep my hands at my side and as neutral an expression as I can. Nigel looks at me, his face visible through a neck hold. 'Wake up, Miles! This is industrial sabotage!' They lead him down the corridor and I can hear him shouting. He's shouting about how they're not fit to call themselves a hospital; they should be subject to a government inquiry and brought down. He calls them *totalitarian*, an impressive syllable count for someone who's being manhandled by two guards. I don't want to think about what they'll do to him. It would take a crate-load of drugs to anaesthetise Nigel. I can hear my name being shouted a couple more times. Then silence.

The nurse looks at me and straightens the duvet. She wants to make sure I'm tucked up. She puts a hand on my forehead. I could swear that she's never looked so proud. She writes a note to ask if she can get me anything. I ask for a coffee. I remind her that it was supposed to come at nine o'clock sharp.

17

THE WIZARD OF BOSCH

The days become not so much days, but sequences of light and dark, and uneventful nothingness. I don't really feel like Miles Platting, founder of Lingua Franca. I feel like a body waiting to be exhumed. Or like Lenin, with my very own box. No one takes hold of my limp hand. No one seems to panic, when it seems for all the world like they should do. It's like they've decided I'm dead already. Nothing they do excites me anymore. The more they feed me the more routine it is. I feel entitled to wake up to a selection of bakery products, as if croissants and scones are the way of the world. It becomes something of an arms race. They increase the rate of croissant supply, they refill my coffee every hour, they want me to do the crossword, as if crosswords are the best thing in the world; they implore the psychiatrist to give me a foot rub, but I don't give it any more importance than getting a pat on the back. They should just plug some hot syrup into my arm.

I lie back and I start to feel it would be nice to walk somewhere. I'd rather go for a walk than lie in bed and stare at the walls, with or without food. The bed opposite remains empty, a Nigel-shaped void. No doubt he's being medically examined or cattle-prodded. The room smells fresher without so many bodies. I begin to lose my sense of time. I couldn't say whether it's Monday or Thursday. I only seem to notice the nurse when she waves a sheet of paper in my face.

You're looking much better!

★   ★   ★

I don't bother to write. I just nod. I ask the nurse if she could restrict my meals, maybe just to one bowl of fruit per day. She smiles as if I'm being polite, and that really, I must be joking. She's never known me to reject the croissants, so she'll believe it when she sees it. She collects some of the mugs and walks to the corridor, no doubt to check if my pizza's ready. I lie with a straight back and close my eyes. There seems to be infinite time, a vast space in which to think. In Stella Artois, there's never enough time; there's always a pitch to prepare, or clients to meet. I lie for a bit longer. I don't suppose there's anything to keep me awake. I feel duty-bound to think about who's at the office, what they're doing and whether they're making any sales. In my absence, and Nigel's derangement, the company has no wheels. It's a stationary train carriage, flat on the tracks; the passengers must wait for the emergency services, who don't speak any language. I find myself looking at the ceiling and projecting onto it my own planetarium. My universe extends from the air vent on the left to the curtain rail on the right. I make up constellations that I give names like The Cobweb and The Moth, imaginary dots that should be worshipped. All hail The Moth. In my universe, nothing needs to get done, and no one needs to go anywhere. I could go to sleep, then wake up and name something else. I could come up with a new alphabet. We could replace the question mark with a §. How does that sound § I start thinking about the cosmos, the universe expanding and what will happen when the sun dies. I wonder what Nigel's evacuation process would be. There will be a scientific name ascribed to whatever's happening. We'll call it heat death, which sounds better than the end of everything. It's hard to think there's a world outside of these walls — a vast, nameless world, with supernovae and dark matter. Maybe in the future, a new

Lingua Franca will colonise the moon and rename each hemisphere after washing machine brands. I want to fly to Bosch.

It gets to the next morning and I'm still in bed. I've got a collection of mugs and a bowl of soggy cereal. Yesterday's croissant has developed a hard, crusted shell. Somewhere in my coat pocket is the envelope containing the verdict on Miles Platting. If I want to read it, I'd have to rummage through my coat, before pulling out the unmarked envelope. I'd have to take a moment to read what Eden's written, and even longer to try and understand it. It would wake me up, no doubt. First I'd feel ashamed; a teardrop would fall upon the page. Then I'd get emotional. I'd start blaming others for everything. I'd rant about how the hospital's done everything wrong. I'd tell them they're contravening X, Y and Z of the UN charter, just like Nigel. I'd pull all the plugs from the medical equipment. I'd throw my half-eaten croissant on the floor. I'd insist upon wearing a robe, rather than the thin patient gown. Nigel and I would find ourselves banished to the laundry room, or made to peel potatoes. I find the energy to lean across and feel inside my coat pocket. I remove the envelope, which is unaddressed, owing to the fact Nigel photocopied the original and gave it to the police. The original must have said, *To Satan*. I rip it open like it's a bank statement or a phone bill. It's a handwritten letter.

For the attention of Miles Platting,

I'm writing this from our laminate living room floor.
I'm lying down, which isn't good for my ribs.

I want to say thank you for giving me the job. Without this experience, I would never have had the confidence to kill myself.

When I got the job, I was so made-up, Miles. We even ordered a takeaway pizza. You like a bit of poverty in your candidates, don't you? You liked it when I said we had a four-year-old daughter and I wanted to be a provider. What did you like about it? Total submissiveness, I guess. A well-fed belly means there's not enough hunger!

But I liked Lingua Franca. Really. I was invisible. I could pick up the phone and not give a fuck about what I was selling. I was Eden from Lingua Franca, but I might as well have been Terry from Bathroom Beauties, or Vince from Kent Drainage. You can't be invisible in Greggs.

You don't know this, but we used to play a game where we'd see who could get the most Michael Jackson songs into our calls. You never seemed to notice, even when I said our offer was a real Thriller. Black or White was a good one. Bad was good. Smooth Criminal was hard. Earth Song impossible.

Do you remember when you made me get you a coffee from the top floor? I made a note of the door code in case I ever wanted to jump from the roof. You should probably relocate that coffee machine.

The only thing I want to say is that I think you should quit Lingua Franca and do what you love. Weren't you once a teacher or something? I find that sad. A real fucking shame.

I've left a folder with all my leads in the drawer. Dudley's a good bet. Call it BNP Paribas.

Thanks again,

Eden

It's not good that I'm staring at the page. It's not good that a teardrop falls and the ink begins to run. I want to go back underground. I want to get back to my hiding place, where no one can see me cry. I stare at the words a little longer, then hold it closer to my chest. I look around and try to regain my cool. I don't want to explain myself in writing. I pull myself under the covers. I close my eyes and think of nothing.

★　★　★

Throughout the morning, they make notes from afar; they don't want to wake me from my dream. They'd prefer to tolerate my self-induced coma from a distance. In the afternoon, they start crowding round me: the nurse takes my pulse and the doctor examines a monitor. I open my eyes and look up in their general direction. I don't stare hard. I'm like the weary victim of a road traffic accident, looking up at two police officers who survey the wreckage. I want to open my mouth but I seem to have developed an in-built mechanism against doing such a thing. I'm not sure I'd even be able to speak properly. I don't feel like an entrepreneur, a man in a suit. I'm present in the room but I wouldn't say I feel alive. I'm part of the lived world, but somewhere else too. I'm a decomposing corpse, consumed by bacteria: asleep, dull . . . nowhere. I can only just feel the tap on my wrist which comes from the nurse. She's holding up a note.

Miles, well done. You're ready to go.

I don't respond. I make no effort to nod, or smile, or write something back. I'm half asleep, half belonging to another space and time, another dimension. I'm aware they're writing notes about me. I know I've become the focus of their efforts. The guard helps me to my feet. It would be difficult to stand without the guard. I know the routine, which helps. I stick out my arms so that they slide into the robe without fuss. I let them straighten my belt and pull the slippers onto my feet. I let them adjust my collar and I notice my name has been etched onto the breast pocket. I know the decorum and the blank face it necessitates. They know what they're doing, too. They're expert professionals when it comes to putting men in robes and handing out candles. I take the candle.

And I smile. I feel like I'm part of something. It feels like the best day of my life.

I'm involved in my own funeral procession, the slow walk from the hospital doors along the path. We follow the candlelit line. We walk under the yellow traffic barrier that looks like a crossbar on a football field, then through the car park and onto the main road. Behind us, the hospital looks like a 1970s university campus, set within countryside. We take care to cross the road, avoiding the oncoming traffic. I wonder if the drivers think we look strange, or maybe they've come to expect people like us. A pedestrian looks in our direction and nods, but he doesn't consider us any more significant than he would a policeman on a horse. There's a small Methodist church with a crowd gathered at the entrance. Someone is shaking a bucket in front of a sign that reads:

Lingua Franca Crisis Appeal

No one shouts anything, which means they shake the bucket hard. I don't recognise any of them. These are just the townspeople, whose sympathies are with Lingua Franca for whatever's happened to our company. Have we been wiped out completely? Am I the mad, sole survivor, bar the blithering Nigel?

It makes me want to walk to the church and find out who's alive. I want to put down my candle and stop the procession. But we keep going. We walk uphill into a stretch of road that feels more remote, lit by grey street lamps, with cattle gates, boring bungalows and hedges. The road narrows into a dark, wooded descent. A railway track dissects the woodland, and we're separated from the track by a small metal fence. Is this where they're going to kill me? Am I going to be tied down and hit by a train to Birdseye? I almost drop the candle. We pass underneath the jagged stonework of a ruined arch. There's an English Heritage sign with a faded imprint: *Furness Abbey*. It needs a new sign, a new name. We walk along a stone path so we don't have to tread on the soft, wet ground. We emerge into an open space, which would once have been a courtyard. Then we stop. I'm here, wherever I'm meant to be. Here we are, in the middle of a ruined abbey, made of sandstone and lit by candles. There are two centurion-style guards on either side of an arch. Someone's leading a slow drum rhythm so that my arrival has some kind of musical accompaniment. Then we're joined by several robed men and women, who emerge as if from the bushes. They position themselves in two distinct groups on either side of a lectern.

251

I'm in the spotlight. The whole congregation is looking at me. At the lectern is a man wearing a white gown that differentiates him from the red robes. He has a rod by his side and a gold chain around his neck. He looks like a wizard. He bangs the rod against the lectern and beckons me forward. The drum continues its steady pound. The wizard presents me with a scroll on which it says:

Miles Platting, you are ready to be discharged. Please sign this consent form and join us in observing a minute's silence to signal the end of your initiation.

They hand me a feathered quill. I look at the wizard, who doesn't look like he'd be happy if I declined the invitation. What's the alternative? I could go back to my hospital bed and lie for a bit longer. I wouldn't get much sleep. I wouldn't be able to forgive myself if I never saw Kendal. And I don't think they'd serve me coffee anymore. I walk to the lectern and the wizard rests the scroll flat. They show me where to print my name. I lean over to write my signature. Miles Platting, signatory. Advocate of the random scroll as presented by our robed friends in the ruined Furness Abbey. There's a gong struck somewhere, which signals the start of the minute's silence.

The wizard closes his eyes. The rest of them link hands like they're remembering a dead person. This is the silent state, remembering its glorious dead, who happen to be alive. Some of them look at me, just in case I'm not observing the silence. The trouble is that I look confused; I don't look solemn enough. I start to relax and pretend I'm one of them. I'm there, standing amid the ruins, with my eyes shut. If I were to shout aloud, it would cause the most extraordinary offence. It would be the worst thing I could do. The worst way to offend silent people is to shout something aloud. I link hands with the wizard. I'm silent too. A trumpet sounds. I almost expect there to be a twelve gunshot salute. The war is over. I'm through to the next stage. I'm brought forward to shake hands with some of the dignitaries, who are essentially just men in robes. The wizard lifts his rod and points it forward. I'm given a nudge and we walk in a procession once more. We follow the line of candles through an enclosed woodland path. They lead me to the little hut on the edge, some kind of gatekeeper's lodge. A little further is a brownstone pub called the Abbey Tavern, but some of its letters are missing so it's spelt *Ab ey Ta ern*, like something in Welsh. The wizard knocks his rod on the wooden door.

We stand around. I'm standing next to a wizard and a group of men in robes. It feels like something from a fable: three little pigs, or something with bears. We wait a little longer until the door opens. I know the face, but the context is wrong. I've never seen Darren in this context. I've never seen him wearing a red robe, and unwilling to speak. I want to say his name. I want to ask him what's inside. He smiles to acknowledge my presence, my turn in the queue, but otherwise he's got a blank expression. If he were going to shout something, now would be the time. He'd say, 'Run away, Miles!' But he doesn't look afraid of anything. He doesn't think I should run away. If he could open his mouth, he'd probably tell me that everything's alright. He wants me to know that he's been inside and everything's okay. They don't bite. They won't boil me in a cauldron or throw me to the lions. Go inside, Miles. You might be surprised at what you find.

Darren walks towards a taxi, which is opened by someone who looks like a druid. Whatever else, Darren's still a boy who'll do what he's told. They probably brainwashed him in twenty seconds. I make a 'call me' gesture, and Darren responds by mimicking a keyboard typist. He looks pretty serious about this. The druid holds open the passenger door. Darren gets inside. Someone will be waiting to order a taxi in the name of Miles Platting.

The wizard holds open the door to the pub. It's my turn. There's no music, no sound of anyone inside. It's just an old stone building and I'm meant to enter. I'm ready to finish my story. I'm ready to get a telling-off, or a certificate of merit. I'm ready for something. I want to go home. Next to the entrance is a black chalkboard. I look at the words and I feel my hand against my heart. The old specials have been erased: you can just about make out *Roast Beef and Hewlett Packard pudding.* What's more important are the new words, in thick white chalk.

The Ministry of Silence.

I look over my shoulder. The druids and wizards know what's coming, even if I don't. They seem to get it. They see my fear.

I breathe out, like I'm standing on the edge of a diving board. And I step into the darkness.

18

THE LEA-RIG

The first thing you notice is the wall of sticky yellow squares, the thousands of words overlaid and repositioned, some in complete sentences, and others a little more monosyllabic. One of them says *Bradford*. Another says *Did you call Rochdale?* Someone will be doing a fantastic trade in Post-It notes. Adhesive is the new gold.

Has anyone got a toothbrush?

It's hard to know what to focus on. My mind elects to focus on whichever words appear first.

How do we put the heating on?

It's a working office, but everyone seems to have gone for lunch, forever. It's a creaking old pub with a hard stone floor. There's a green recycling box with lots of empty beer bottles. The dining area has wooden slab benches and a row of computers. On the table are notepads, calculators and cardboard boxes containing *#ZipIt* T-shirts, each with a finger pressed against a pair of lips. The bar is unattended and all the stools are tucked in. I could pull myself a pint, but there would probably be consequences. In my red robe, I almost feel like a responsible adult. I enter the back room and at the other end of the long table is Kendal. I'm smiling inside, even if I don't want to show it. I want to hold Kendal, and walk together in the cold. I want to sit by the water's edge and pretend the Devonshire Dock Hall is the Ponte Vecchio. I want to book our flights to Costa Rica and get Ptolemy a pet passport. All of this seems possible. Kendal's typing while looking at her computer screen; she doesn't look up. She presses another few keys then hits what I imagine to be the 'enter' key. Now she's looking at me. She gestures for where she wants me to sit. Behind Kendal is a projector screen with a black background and white text.

Good evening, Miles. Please take a seat.

I sit and look at my wife, who maintains a professional, workaday face. I'm the one millionth person she's seen today, and I'm no more special than the last. In front of me there's a computer monitor with the cursor flashing at the start of an unwritten sentence. I've got a wireless keyboard and a lamp in case I need to see what I'm typing. Kendal has a clicker; when she presses it, the projector turns to another slide. It displays a Ministry of Silence logo accompanied by blue swirls. It says the company is headquartered at the Abbey Tavern, Barrow-in-Furness.

The Ministry of Silence was founded with the objective of restoring traditional place names to branded settlements throughout the United Kingdom.

The next slide is a Soviet-style painting of a woman calling aloud. The text appears from her mouth.

The Ministry endorses the concept of silent living, whereby spoken language is rejected in favour of non-verbal communication and British Sign Language.

She presses the clicker and the next slide comes up. The picture is a map of the British Isles with various red dots.

Already, the Ministry has created volunteer centres across eight UK settlements. Local activists have established Quiet Zones across public spaces, offering a place of thought, respite and an unequivocal rejection of the commercialisation of language.

She flicks to a slide that displays the 1970s red-brick hospital I've just escaped from.

Our Wordsworth Institute, formerly Furness Hospital, is a rehabilitation centre in Barrow-in-Furness. The Institute promotes a silent culture among its patients, who become silent ambassadors in their community.

Next we see the *ZipIt* logo, the shushing lips and the red background colour.

Our #ZipIt campaign has achieved a significant digital penetration across multiple channels.

The next slide features a mass of people in different work attire: nurses, firefighters and men in cotton shirts. They're all looking at the camera, holding signs that read *Quiet please*. Kendal flicks to what I expect is the final slide: a contract, which requires my digital signature.

The Ministry of Silence is pleased to confirm that your rehabilitation programme is complete. Please be advised that we require your written consent before you're officially discharged.

She flicks between more slides, showing me the terms and conditions. There are lots of conditions. I nod my head and it feels like this is all I'm capable of doing. My neck is a loose spring. I can only nod. She starts typing; she's going off-piste.

Come on, Miles. It's time to go home.

She smiles as she types.

You can redeem yourself, Miles. You can become Miles the Great, not Miles the Terrible. Miles Platting, language killer, Miles Platting, language . . . saviour.

She looks at me like it's my turn. I look at the computer monitor. I feel like I'm sitting in front of a steering wheel and I've forgotten how to drive. What must I look like? I must look lost. I start to type, making a couple of mistakes along the way, which means I press the backspace. I eventually manage to compose a few words:

What's with all the robes?

It's a good question, judging by the speed at which she types. I deserve an instant reply. She presses the enter key and sits back in her chair.

I just wanted to fuck with you.

She's smiling now. For the first time, she looks like Kendal, my mad Kendal, the one I love. She might be silent but I can see what she's saying. I want to go home. I don't want to sit in a pub in Barrow-in-Furness in my red robe. I want to see Ptolemy, my fortress in the former Milton Keynes, and whatever remains of Lingua Franca. I want to do what Kendal says. I want to exchange the habits of a lifetime for something more tangible: love.

I look for a pen, then realise a pen isn't what I'm looking for. I look for the cursor, then move my mouse so I can aim for the dotted line. I click, then find the cursor exactly where I wanted. Then I press each letter at a time.

MILES

What is Miles? Where did my name come from? I never asked my mother where it came from, and what it even means.

PLATTING

And what is Miles Platting? It sounds like *plotting*, or something to do with hairstyling: *to plait*. I've never really given it any thought. It has a history, my name, and I probably ought to know. I press the enter key and I look up in the hope I've done a good thing. I want a gold star. Kendal closes the laptop lid. She's done. She's finished her PowerPoint routine and now it's time to relax. She rises from her seat and stretches her arms. I make an expressive gesture with my hands, like I'm saying *what now?*

We walk into the dining area and she holds my hand. From the window we can see the moonlight and some of the ruins. We can see the train line where the freights pass. We can have our own lock-in. We can drink the wine and whiskey and go for a candlelit walk. We can speak our own language. We have what we need, and we need nothing else. She walks behind the bar without asking me to follow. I wonder what's coming next. It could be anything. I'm intent on smiling — over-smiling — so that she knows I'm happy with everything. She kneels beside the fridge and then stands, holding two wine glasses with a bottle under her arm: a bottle of Bordeaux. She opens it, then pours a small drop. Her expression says *do you want to try it, sir?* I wave a hand like I'm saying *no, it's fine.* She nods, as if to say *very well, sir.* She pours the rest. She fills two glasses and we stand together and clink. Here's to life, to Miles and Kendal. We can speak our own language, and we need nothing else.

19

DAWN

<u>A special announcement from the
Lingua Franca team</u>

Dear Sir/Madam,
We're excited to tell you about a new
special offer that won't cost you a penny.
Lingua Franca is partnering with the
Ministry of Silence to restore traditional
place names to communities across the
United Kingdom. For no cost at all, we
will partner with your town to dismantle
all branded signage and reinstate a
traditional name of your choice.

How does it work?

The Ministry of Silence has created a
community trust fund backed by crowd-
funding and private equity investment
which will enable Lingua Franca to buy
out the contracts for each of its 69
sponsored settlements in the UK. Our
long-term vision is to restore every

*branded town and city in the country to
its rightful name. We hope that you will
join us in this endeavour.*

Find out more

Click here to unsubscribe

Gravesend is interested. Peterborough has
woken from its sleep. Grimsby wants to know
what Cleethorpes thinks about it. Dorking is
coming round. And Yeovil too. Liverpool
knew the whole thing was stupid all along.

We stand around in a circle without saying
anything, like something from a Buddhist
retreat. The subject is Croydon. On the
whiteboard, Head of Brand writes a list of
everything Croydon's ever been called.
Croeas . . . Deanas . . . Croindone . . . Crogdene . . . Croydon . . . Carphone Warehouse.
It's more than likely that Croydon will insist
upon *Croydon*, but they're free to consider
the ancient alternatives, the Roman, Bry-
thonic, Middle English or Old Norse. They
might be feeling Pictish. Localisation writes
on her Etch A Sketch, then raises it aloft.

Croydon's better than Crogdene.

Croydon it is.

It must be the seventh *expression session* that Nigel's missed. The Ministry have advised us that his rehabilitation is incomplete. Every time he gets better, he allows his anger to overcome him. He shouts about terms and conditions, and how everything's a disgrace. Then he goes back to the start. He's not very good at the wire buzzer game. He doesn't understand the process. The rest of us understood what was required. That's how we got through the storm, and the silent rehabilitation.

Luton's better than Loitone. And definitely better than Lucozade.

In time, the perception of Lingua Franca will be different. Lingua Franca, specialists in silence. No headsets, no telephones. Every item of business conducted in British Sign Language and the written word. Thought leaders. Standard bearers. We could tell you about our behavioural framework with our bare hands.

They all type at once, and we keep them sane by letting them listen to classical music — nothing with lyrics, unless it's Ronan Keating's 'You Say It Best When You Say Nothing At All': our joke song. Eden was polite enough to categorise his leads into 'hot' and 'cold'. Basingstoke is hot. Plymouth is cold. Wycombe is a 'messer'. We've contacted the hot leads to announce that we won't be selling naming rights anymore. We're Lingua Franca, language restorationists. Look on our works, ye Mighty, and rejoice.

The English language belongs to all of us.
It is the property of the heart.

Darren's a good writer. A better writer than he ever was a talker. He likes to write down his thoughts and stick them on the wall.

Though we speak in different accents,
and differ in our diction, all of us are
fluent in the language of silence.

Darren leans onto the whiteboard, the column marked *Eden*. He writes some Roman numerals in permanent ink. Number eleven, Eden's last sales figure. It'll stay there for as long as we're here.

If Nigel ever comes back, I'll be ready with the graphs. Our key performance indicators have been met, Nigel. We have a mass-market audience. Our social channels get something like two hundred thousand subscribers. We run successful campaigns with names like *Hush*. A generation of young people read our newsletter, organise vigils, raise funds, spread the word (in silence) and dance in silent discos. Affinity is up. Advocacy is up. Online sentiment is positive. In Barrow-in-Furness there are hundreds of volunteers working on the ground. In Milton Keynes there are *#ZipIt* logos hanging from the lamp posts all the way up Midsummer Boulevard, like something from a police state where the population worship a pair of lips. We're doing great, Nigel. Just relax.

Ptolemy and I have a new housemate called Kendal. It feels like a different house. We took down the iron bars and the CCTV. The metal spikes are stubborn, but we've found a spike specialist. The gravel's gone; we've laid grass and planted some daffodils in the front. The anti-climb paint is chipping away. We use the panic room for storage. We've unplugged the burglar alarm so Ptolemy can explore at night without fear of tripping the lasers. I let Kendal manage the bookshelves. She wants to read everything ever written. She likes to pin poems on the wall, so I can read e.e. cummings while washing my face. We've both become better at drawing. Yesterday I found a note on the pillow which said *I love you*. The *love* was a red crayon heart. We write about everything. We write about our day, and what we're eating for dinner. We write about how we're feeling, what's making us sad and what we love about one another. We write about hospitals, primary schools and 'Outstanding' Ofsted reports. We write about our baby, and toys, and how Ptolemy will cope. All we need is a name.

Acknowledgements

A big thank you to Ben Casey and The Chase agency for the beautiful cover art on the Legend Press edition.

Thank you to Lauren Parsons, the Legend Press team and James Wills at Watson Little.

Mad props to Mark Gill and Baldwin Li for their omniscient divinity.

To the First Lady Sarah Jack. And Tariq Desai of no fixed address.

To the Thacker-Leicester dynasty, Chairman Meow, and my Iceman incarcerated.

To the 8.04 from Kentish Town to Bromley South.

And last but not least, to the people of Birdseye.